Only a DUKE WOULD *Dare*

Seductive Scoundrels, Book Two

COLLETTE CAMERON

Blue Rose Romance®
Portland, Oregon

Sweet-to-Spicy Timeless Romance®

ONLY A DUKE WOULD DARE
Seductive Scoundrels
Copyright © 2018 Collette Cameron
Cover Design by: Kim Killion

Blue Rose Romance®
8420 N Ivanhoe # 83054
Portland, Oregon 97203

ISBN Paperback: 9781954307551
ISBN eBook: 9781954307544
www.collettecameron.com

"I'm not so foxed that I don't know what to do with a beautiful woman in my arms."
Duke of Sutcliffe.

"Delightful, dazzling, and oh-so delicious."
~ Cheryl Bolen *NYT Bestselling* Author.

Other Collette Cameron Books

Seductive Scoundrels
A Diamond for a Duke
Only a Duke Would Dare
A December with a Duke
What Would a Duke Do?
Wooed by a Wicked Duke
Duchess of His Heart
Never Dance with a Duke
Earl of Wainthorpe
Earl of Scarborough
Wedding her Christmas Duke
The Debutante and the Duke
Earl of Keyworth

Coming soon in the series!
How to Win A Duke's Heart
Loved by a Dangerous Duke
When a Duke Loves a Lass

Check out Collette's Other Series

Daughters of Desire (Scandalous Ladies)

Highland Heather Romancing a Scot

The Blue Rose Regency Romances:

The Culpepper Misses

Castle Brides

The Honorable Rogues®

Heart of a Scot

Collections

Lords in Love

The Honorable Rogues® Books 1-3

The Honorable Rogues® Books 4-6

Seductive Scoundrels Series Books 1-3

Seductive Scoundrels Series Books 4-6

The Blue Rose Regency Romances-

The Culpepper Misses Series 1-2

Dedication

Dedicated to every girl or woman

who also reads while watching television . . .

Yes, it's possible to keep track of both stories.

Acknowledgements

A special thanks to Kim Killion for ONLY A DUKE WOULD DARE'S gorgeous cover, Period Images for the exclusive image on the cover, to my daughter Brianna for helping me pick the cover models, my talented and oh-so organized assistants CJ and DF who do soooo much behind the scenes for me, and my editors Kathryn Davis and Emilee Bowling for polishing my story until it dazzles. A humble thank you to Cheryl Bolen for her cover quote, and thanks too, to Lana Lee Harmon-Bury for suggesting Acheron's name, and to Paula Adams, Liz Mackman, Keri Smith, Virginia Smith, and Sherri Jordan-Stephens for helping me name The Blue Rose Inn at Essex Crossings. You are brilliant!

Colchester, Essex England
Late June 1809

Twilight's gloom lengthened the shadows in the old cemetery as Theadosia—humming *Robin Adair*, a Scottish love song certain to vex her father—wended her way through the grave markers and the occasional gangly rose bush or shrubbery in need of pruning.

Having lived at the rectory her entire life, she found the graveyard neither frightening nor eerie. Those lying in eternal rest included a brother who'd died in infancy, several townspeople she'd known, and even a few gentry and nobles for whom Father had performed funerals. As children, she and her sisters and brother had frolicked amongst the stones and statuary, playing hide and seek and other games.

Situated on the east side of All Saints Church to catch the rising sun each morning, the churchyard provided a convenient, often-used shortcut to the parsonage's back entrance.

"Why?"

A deep, anguished whisper drifted across the expanse.

Though she didn't believe in ghosts and despite her velvet spencer, an icy prickle zipped down her spine, causing the hairs on her arms to stand at attention.

Lifting her robin's egg blue chintz gown with one hand, she paused and glanced around but saw nothing out of the ordinary. A plump, greyish-brown rabbit, enjoying a snack before finding its way home for the evening, watched her with wary, black-button eyes. After another moment of studying the familiar landscape, Theadosia continued on her way.

She must've imagined the voice.

The wind had whipped up in the last few minutes. Sometimes, the two ancient oaks acting as sentinels at the cemetery entrance groaned in such a way that the swaying branches sounded as if they were moaning in protest.

Perhaps Jessica's chickens had made an odd noise, Theadosia reassured herself as the wind lashed her skirts around her ankles. Situated on the other side of the parish where the vegetable and flower gardens were, the chickens often made odd sounding cackles and clucks.

The empty basket that had held the chicken soup and bread she'd delivered to the sick Ulrich family this afternoon banged against her thigh as she resumed her humming, even daring to sing a line from the song since she'd inspected the area and her parents weren't present to chastise her.

"Yet him I lov'd so well—"

"Why'd you do it?"

The same tormented baritone rasped through the burial ground once more.

That, by Jehoshaphat, she had *not* imagined.

She stopped again and turned in a slow circle, trying to peer around the greeneries and headstones. Many were large and ornate, and she couldn't see past the nearby stone markers.

"I jus' want to know why."

The rabbit froze for a second before darting into the hedgerow.

A shiver tiptoed across Theadosia's shoulders, and she swallowed against a flicker of fear.

Come now, Theadosia Josephine Clarice Brentwood. You are made of sterner stuff.

Besides, ghosts didn't slur their words. At least, she didn't think so.

Gathering her resolve, she pulled herself to her full five-feet-nine inches and called, "Who's there?"

She squinted into the dusk. The voice had come from the graveyard's far side. The side reserved for aristocrats and nobles.

Another wind gust whistled through the dogwoods and flowering cherry trees bordering the cemetery's north side and tugged at the brim of her new straw bonnet. She held it tightly to keep it in place.

Once more, a mumbled phrase—or perhaps a sob this time—followed on the tails of the crisp breeze.

What distraught soul had ventured into the graveyard at this hour?

Visitors usually came 'round in the morning or afternoon. On occasion, they even picnicked amongst those who'd gone before them. Superstitions and unwarranted fears usually kept mourners away as darkness descended, however.

Whoever the person was, they were in distress for certain, and Theadosia's compassionate nature demanded she offer to help. Slipping the basket over her forearm, she strode in the direction she thought she'd heard the voice coming from. As she rounded a weeping angel tombstone, so old and discolored the writing could scarce be read anymore, she skidded to a halt.

A man—a very startlingly attractive man—lay amongst the dead.

Rather, surrounded by a low, pointed iron fence, he lounged atop what must be his greatcoat, his back against a six-foot marble marker. Even in death, the dukes and duchesses of Sutcliffe, as well as their immediate kin, kept themselves separated from the commoners—those they deemed beneath their illustrious blue-blooded touch.

That was what the locals claimed, in any event.

She'd never found the Sutcliffes uppity or unfriendly. A mite stuffy and formal, for certain, as nobility often were, but never unkind. Not that she'd spent a great deal of time in any of their company.

Preposterously long legs crossed at the ankles and his raven hair disheveled as if he been running his fingers through it, the gentleman took a lengthy swig from a green bottle.

Whisky.

Father would kick up a fierce dust if he found out.

The tanned column of the man's throat, a startling contrast to the snowfall of a neckcloth beneath his chin, worked as he swallowed again.

Something had him overwrought.

As he lowered his arm, she widened her eyes.

He's home!

Theadosia's heartbeat stuttered a trifle as she

raked her gaze over Victor, the Duke of Sutcliffe. Though she hadn't seen him in three and one-half years, she easily recognized his grace.

A wave of sympathy swept her.

She also knew what tormented him.

His father's suicide.

'Twas his father's grave he sat upon.

Eyes closed, his sable lashes fanned against his sculpted cheekbones, the duke lifted the bottle once more.

"You didn't even leave a note telling us why."

Theadosia wasn't supposed to know the reason the seventh duke had hanged himself. Such things were never discussed except behind closed doors. Her Father, the rector of All Saint's Church, frowned upon gossip or tattle of any sort.

What she thought surely must be a tear leaked from the corner of his grace's eye. His obvious grief tore at her soft heart.

She shouldn't.

Her parents wouldn't approve. In fact, Father absolutely forbade it.

Biting her lower lip, Theadosia closed her eyes for an instant.

She really, *really* should not.

But she would.

She couldn't bear to see the duke's suffering.

Reservations resolutely, if somewhat unwisely, tamped down, she passed through the gaping gate.

"Your father had stomach cancer. I overheard Papa telling Mama one day after your father . . . That is, after he died. Papa felt guilty for not telling you and your mother, but the duke swore him to secrecy, and of course he had no idea your father would . . ." Why people choose to keep such serious matters from their families boggled the mind.

Eyelids flying open, his grace jerked upright.

His hypnotic gaze snared hers, and yes, moisture glinted there.

Her heart gave a queer leap.

She remembered his vibrant eyes, the shade somewhere between silver and pewter with the merest hint of ocean blue around the irises. Not cold eyes, despite their cool colors. No, his eyes brimmed with intelligence and usually kindness, and they crinkled at the corners when he laughed. He'd laughed often as a young man; her brother James had been one of his constant companions whenever his grace was in residence at Ridgewood Court.

"Cancer?" His eyelids drifted shut again, and he nodded. "*Ahhh.*"

That single word revealed he understood.

Mayhap he'd find a degree of peace now.

"Thank you for telling me," he said.

"I've always thought you should know."

He should have been told years ago.

Bracing himself on his father's headstone, the duke maneuvered to his feet. With the whisky bottle dangling from one hand, he squinted as if trying to focus his bleary-eyed gaze.

"Theadosia?" Uncertainty raised his deep voice higher on the last syllable as he looked her up and down, an appreciative gleam in his eye.

"Thea, is that truly you?"

Only her siblings and dearest friends called her Thea.

His surprise was warranted. Mama said Theadosia had been a late bloomer. She'd almost despaired of developing proper womanly curves.

She bobbed a half curtsy and grinned.

"It is indeed, Your Grace. I'm all grown up now." At sixteen—embarrassingly infatuated with him and possessing a figure a broomstick might envy—she'd believed herself a woman full grown. Time had taught her otherwise.

The duke's extended absence had caused a great deal of conjecture and speculation, and many, including her, wondered if he'd ever return to Colchester.

She so yearned to ask why he'd come back after all this time, but etiquette prohibited any such thing.

He hitched his mouth into a sideways smile as his gaze roved over her.

"I'll say you are. And you've blossomed into quite a beauty too. Always knew you would."

He'd noticed the thin, gawky girl with the blotchy complexion? She'd barely been able to cobble two words together in his presence.

A delicious sensation, sweet and warm, similar to fresh pulled taffy, budded behind her breastbone. She shouldn't be flattered at his drunken ravings. In fact, she ought to reproach him for his brazen compliment. After all, he was a known rapscallion, a man about town, "a philandering rake," Papa avowed. Nevertheless, it wasn't every day a devilishly handsome duke called her beautiful.

Actually, rarely did anyone remark on her features.

Her father frowned on the praise of outward appearances, which explained why the gentlemen he'd encouraged her to turn her attention to couldn't be said to be pleasing to the eye.

The Lord tells us not to consider appearance or height, but to look at a man's heart, he admonished Thea and her sister regularly.

Easier to do if the man didn't boast buck teeth, a hooked nose to rival a parrot's beak, or a propensity to sweat like a race horse: the last three curates, respectively.

His grace, on the other hand, was most pleasing to

the eye. Oh, indeed he most assuredly was.

Deliciously tall—perfect for a woman of her height—and classically handsome, his face all aristocratic planes and angles. Even the severe blade of his nose and the lashing of his black brows spoke of generations of refined breeding.

Papa, a plain featured, thick man himself, had married a Scottish beauty. It truly wasn't fair he demanded otherwise of his offspring.

Why couldn't he find a good-hearted *and* somewhat attractive man to woo his middle daughter?

Was that too much to ask?

But she knew why.

Because a handsome face *had* turned his eldest daughter Althea's head, and she'd run off with a performer from the Summer Faire. For the past two and a half years, Papa had forbidden anyone to utter her name.

Theadosia's heart ached anew. How she longed for word from her beloved sister, but if Althea had ever sent a letter, Papa hadn't mentioned it. His blasted pride wouldn't permit it.

Even Mama, more tolerant and good-natured than Papa, didn't dare remind him what the Good Book said about pride and forgiveness.

Sighing, Theadosia ran her gaze over the duke again.

James would be delighted when he came up from London next.

"A pleasure to see you again, Miss Thea."

A charming smile flashed across his grace's noble countenance as he bent into a wobbly gallant's bow— dropping the whisky bottle and nearly falling onto his face for his efforts. He chuckled at his own clumsiness.

She dropped the basket and rushed forward to brace him with one hand on his broad—*very broad*— shoulder and the other on his solid chest. Being a prudent miss, she dismissed the electric jolt sluicing up both arms. This was not the time for missish shyness or false pretenses of demureness.

Imagine the scandal if his grace were found insensate, reeking of whisky, atop his father's grave? This was *not* the homecoming she'd imagined for him over the years.

"Do have a care, sir, or you will crack your skull." Supporting his great weight, for his form wasn't that of simpering dandy, but a man accustomed to physical exertion, she slanted him a sideways glance. "I believe you've over-indulged."

A great deal, truth to tell.

"How ever will you manage your way home to Ridgewood Court?"

"The same way I came to be here in this dreary place." Giving her a boyish sideways grin, he waggled his fingers in the general direction of the lane. "I shall walk, fair maiden."

"I think not. 'Tis a good mile, and you're in no condition to make the hike."

"Do you fret for me, Thea?" His rich voice had gone all low and raspy.

He lowered his head and pressed his nose into her neck as he wrapped his arms around her and pulled her flush with his body.

Shouldn't she be offended or afraid?

Yet she wasn't either.

"*Mmm*, you smell good. Like sunshine and

honeysuckle."

He smelled of strong spirits, horse, and sandalwood. And something else she couldn't quite identify. She couldn't very well lean in and sniff to determine what the scent was, as he'd boldly ventured to do.

His grace inhaled a deep breath, another unnerving sound she couldn't identify reverberating in his throat. "Intoxicating," he rumbled against her neck, his lips tickling the sensitive flesh.

Trying—*unsuccessfully*—to ignore the heady pleasure of being near him, Theadosia tilted her head away whilst bracing her hands against the wall that was his chest.

"You are the one who's intoxicated and don't know what you're saying."

Why must she sound breathless?

The exertion of holding him upright. That must be it.

"Your Grace." She gave that unyielding wall a shove. "You must release me before someone sees us."

Not much chance of that with evening's mantle

descending, but it was foolish to tempt Providence.

"I'm not so foxed that I don't know what to do with a beautiful woman in my arms."

There was the rogue Papa had warned her and Jessica about.

The sharp retort meant to remind him of his place was replaced by a sigh as his lips brushed hers.

Once.

Twice.

And again, with more urgency.

Did she resist as a proper, moral cleric's daughter ought to? Summon outrage or indignation? Even the merest bit?

Lord help her, no.

Was she as wanton as Althea?

Did such wickedness run in families?

She stood there, ensconced in his arms, and let him kiss her. She may have even kissed him back, but her mind was such a muddle of delicious sensations, akin to floating on a fluffy cloud, she couldn't be certain.

His soft yet firm lips tasted of whisky and

something more.

Passion, perhaps?

"And here, Mr. Leadford, are the church burial grounds."

"We have graves dating over two hundred years ago, prior to the erection of All Saint Church's current buildings."

Her father's voice, drifting to her from several rows away, succeeded in yanking Theadosia back to earth and apparently sobered his grace as well. At once she disengaged herself from his embrace.

She risked much if she were caught. Everything, in fact. Papa had expressly prohibited his remaining daughters to be unchaperoned in the company of males over the age of twelve.

"I'm confident you'll feel as blessed as I do as you assist in the shepherding of my flock." Pride resonated in Papa's deep voice, quite useful for his booming Sunday morning sermons. "I confess, I've been a trifle lax in my paperwork the past few months. The last curate was a Godsend when it came to organization, record keeping, and correspondences. Such matters are not amongst my strengths."

"Fret not, for those are my fortes as well, Mr. Brentwood," a pleasant but unfamiliar voice replied."

"I'm well pleased to hear it," her father replied.

Another new curate?

That made four in as many years. A quartet of unattached males seeking a modest woman of respectable birth to take to wife. Thus far, she and her younger sister, Jessica, had been spared.

Fortunately, each of the former curates had selected a docile—*ambitious*—parishioner from the congregation to wed before moving on to their own parish.

Unfortunately, All Saint's Church had few unassuming, unattached misses of marriageable age left.

"Thea . . .?"

The duke reached for her again.

"*Shh!*"

She pressed her gloved fingers against his lips, and he promptly gripped her hand and pressed a kiss to her wrist.

"Stop that," she whispered, tugging her hand away whilst silently ordering the fluttering in her tummy to cease.

"My father's near. I *cannot* be found in a compromising position with you. He'll be livid. *Please*. Let go, sir."

She'd be disowned on the spot. Cast out and shunned. Her name never uttered by her family again. She'd never see them again either. Ever.

Imagining Papa's infuriated reaction sent a tremor down her spine.

Even in his stupor, the duke must've sensed her fright and urgency, for he released her at once and put a respectable distance between them.

"I'd prefer you call me Sutcliffe or Victor."

What did she owe that honor to?

Sutcliffe she might consider, but she could not use his given name, except in her mind. Only the closest of relatives and friends might address him by anything other than his title.

As Theadosia stepped even farther away and righted her bonnet, her foot struck the whisky bottle.

Her gaze fell on the forgotten basket outside the fence. *Bother and rot.* She could only pray her father's tour didn't include this portion of the grounds.

An exclamation, followed by a flurry of whispers, made her whirl toward the lane paralleling the churchyard.

The elderly Nabity sisters, bony arms entwined and heads bent near, stood on the pathway.

What had they seen?

Theadosia closed her eyes.

Pray God, only her conversing with the duke, a respectable distance between them, and nothing more.

His grace turned to where she peered so intently. Wearing a silly, boyish grin, he bowed once more, this time with more control, though he swayed on his feet in imitation of a sapling battered by a winter tempest.

"Good afternoon, dear ladies. I do hope I'll have the pleasure of speaking with you after services Sunday. I've missed your keen wit and your delicious seed cake these many years."

In unison, their sagging chins dropped nearly to their flat-as-a-washboard chests, before they bobbed their heads in affirmation and, tittering in the irksome manner of green schoolgirls, toddled off. Probably to make their famed confection.

"I think you said that just so they'd make you seed cake." The rascal.

"You've found me out."

An unabashed grin quirked his mouth, and she pressed her lips together, remembering the heady sensation of his mouth on hers.

"Theadosia? What the devil goes on here?"

*P**apa.*

Stifling the unladylike oath she wasn't even supposed to know, let alone think or say, Theadosia shot the duke a now-look-what-you've-done glance. Papa would be horrified to know what naughtiness she'd learned from her closest friends over the years.

Where they came by the knowledge she had no idea, nor did she want to know.

His grace had the good sense to arrange his face into a solemn mien, though she swore mischief danced in his half-closed eyes. Hard to tell with the fading light, however.

Affecting nonchalance despite her runaway pulse

and the fear of discovery tightening her tummy, she summoned a sunny smile and edged forward until her gown covered the forgotten bottle of "devil's drink", as her father called whisky.

"Papa. Look who's returned to Colchester."

She swept her hand toward the duke.

Papa's expression remained severe as he took the duke's measure.

Not good.

Perchance if she distracted her father by mentioning his latest fundraising venture to improve All Saints, he wouldn't become angry at what he was sure to deem her most indecorous behavior.

"His grace was telling me how eager he is to hear you preach this Sunday, and he said he'd be honored to contribute the balance needed for the new chamber organ. You'll be able to order it now. Isn't that marvelous? Imagine how lovely the music echoing in the sanctuary will be every Sunday and at Christmastide."

One of Papa's stern brows twitched in interest.

Perfect. He'd taken the bait.

Now to gently reel him in.

Contriving her most grateful smile, she caught the duke's eye.

Distinct amusement and a mite of 'what-are-you-about-now?' danced along the edges of his face.

"And his grace suggested it only fitting that the choir have new cassocks and surplices. He insists upon covering their cost as well. Isn't it a blessing?"

Would God judge her for fibbing?

He well should.

Even if the lies were well intended?

Or contrived out of dread?

More on point and of greater worry now, would the duke deny her declarations?

The chamber organ's cost was most dear. For over two years the congregation had fund-raised, but Papa said they still hadn't collected half the necessary monies. To volunteer the duke's purse was beyond the pale, but she truly must divert Papa from jumping to the wrong—*actually accurate*—conclusion.

Why had she been so impulsive?

She should've alerted her father that someone was

in distress in the cemetery, and not taken it upon herself to intervene.

But then she wouldn't have been kissed until she forgot she was a reverend's daughter.

"Naturally, if there is to be a new organ, the choir is deserving of new robes," the Duke of Sutcliffe murmured in a droll tone.

Was that a wink, the brazen bounder?

Had Papa seen?

Her father's speculative gaze flicked between her and the duke, then the ostentatious marker behind his grace before his features relaxed, and he offered his version of a sanctimonious smile: mouth closed, lips tilted up a fraction, his expression benign.

Placing his palms together in a prayer-like pose, he dipped his gray-streaked head the merest bit.

"Your benevolence is much appreciated, Your Grace. I'm sure our Lord is as delighted as I that you've chosen to follow your parents' practices of regular church attendance and generous patronage to the parish."

"As you say, Mr. Brentwood."

His grace inclined his head, all traces of his earlier boyishness and inebriation now concealed. Either the duke was practiced at artifice or he was a superb actor. Or mayhap he hadn't been as tippled as she believed.

Thank goodness he hadn't disputed her grand declaration about his generous donation.

Later she'd have to apologize and beg his forgiveness for her duplicity.

"Permit me to introduce our newest curate, Your Grace." Papa indicated the amiable clergyman who hadn't stopped smiling since he'd rounded the tombstone. "Mr. Leadford, this is His Grace, Victor, Duke of Sutcliffe, and my daughter, Theadosia. Sir, Theadosia, this is Mr. Hector Leadford."

Possessing piercing blue eyes in an unremarkable, but kind face, Mr. Leadford bowed.

Something about him raised her nape hairs, but she couldn't put her finger on what.

"Your Grace. Miss Brentwood. It is a pleasure to make both of your acquaintances."

His gaze lingered a mite longer than entirely professional, or necessary, on Theadosia, and distinct appreciation glinted in his striking eyes.

Mayhap his interest is what she's sensed.

"I hope you enjoy our township, Mr. Leadford, and that you'll feel at home here very soon."

Theadosia returned his smile, mindful to keep hers polite but slightly distant lest she encourage his regard. Exactly as she and Jessica had been taught to do. In Papa's view, encouraging male attention was akin to running naked through Colchester banging on a drum.

The only man's esteem she desired—had ever desired—stood but a few feet from her. A man far beyond her reach, she knew full well. A man she measured all others against, which was truly unfair, for it was impossible for anyone else to compete with the duke. In her mind, at least.

A man whose elevated station required Papa's deference, but also a man of whom her father would never approve. The Duke of Sutcliffe was precisely the kind of man Papa disdained—one who lived for pleasure alone, or so her father claimed. Honestly, she didn't think he admired anyone other than clergymen, and none other would do for his daughters.

The wind whistled between the tombstones, and the duke leaned down to retrieve his coat and hat. Dusk was fully upon them now, and the candlelight shining from the windows of the parsonage lent a welcoming glow to the graveyard.

Theadosia sent him a short, speaking glance before lowering her attention to her feet in what Papa would assume was diffident behavior, but was, in fact, the only hint she could give the Duke of Sutcliffe.

She couldn't move lest the bottle be revealed.

If Papa discovered his grace had been imbibing hard spirits whilst on Church grounds, he'd have an apoplexy. It wouldn't do for her father to ban the most powerful man in the county from All Saints Church. Nor would it do for Papa to offend the newly returned duke. And it most assuredly would not do for her to be caught hiding the bottle.

Papa's wrath, though rare, was terrifying.

Sutcliffe draped his coat over his forearm and, holding his beaver hat between his forefinger and thumb, pondered his father's grave.

"I beg your indulgence, though the hour grows

late. I would appreciate a few more moments' privacy."

Papa pressed his lips together in sympathetic understanding and nodded.

"Yes, of course. Mr. Leadford, let's enjoy a glass of port in the salon before supper, shall we? I do believe I smelled chicken fricassee and cherry pie earlier." He waved the other clergyman before him and paused to glance over his shoulder. "I look forward to seeing you and your mother Sunday morning."

"It was a pleasure to make your acquaintance," Mr. Leadford repeated as he bent to retrieve the discarded basket. He'd clearly discerned who it belonged to, and it appeared he intended to be the gallant.

Beaming his approval, Papa didn't even ask why she'd abandoned the basket.

Praise the Almighty for small favors.

As soon as her father faced away, Mr. Leadford's attention sank to her bosoms, then lower still, and her stomach clenched.

Now her nape hairs stood straight up and wiggled

about, and she resisted the urge to retreat from his frank perusal.

Pray to God Mr. Leadford wasn't Papa's choice of a husband for her.

At twenty, Theadosia couldn't hope to continue to claim she was too young to wed, and that Papa intended to select a man of his own ilk for his younger two daughters became more apparent every day.

It was her own fault she wanted more than spiritual companionship.

No, her friend, Nicolette, was partially to blame for sneaking Theadosia romance novels to read. They lay tucked beneath a floorboard under the bed she and Jessica shared. Nicolette had promised to lend her latest books when Theadosia saw her next.

God help her if Papa ever learned of them. He wasn't a harsh or unreasonable man; he simply had a very strict moral code he vehemently enforced. More so since Althea had eloped.

Sutcliffe inclined his head before turning his attention to Theadosia and bidding her farewell with a nod and a penetrating look.

"Miss Brentwood."

"Your Grace." She curtsied but didn't move.

Papa was too close.

Without a doubt, though evening was upon them, he'd see the bright green bottle.

"Theadosia, why are you standing there?" Giving her the gimlet eye, her father pressed his mouth into a stern line. "His grace requested privacy. Hurry inside. Your mother and sister need your assistance with supper. Come along now."

Speaking low to Mr. Leadford, Papa angled in the direction of the Church, and the duke seized the opportunity to drop his hat—right at her feet.

"I beg your pardon."

His mouth twitched with concealed amusement.

She neatly stepped aside as he squatted and retrieved the hat whilst tucking the bottle beneath the folds of his coat with his other hand.

"Oh, well done, you," she whispered, quite enjoying their colluding.

"Thank you for saving me much embarrassment." His confidential tone heated her to her toes. "And for telling me about my father's illness."

"Theadosia Josephine Clarice!" More than impatience tinged Papa's voice. "Stop dawdling."

Had he discerned her interest in the duke?

"I'm coming, Papa."

"Mr. Brentwood?"

His grace stared past her head.

Papa turned, one grizzled brow cocked in inquiry.

"Yes?"

"I can see that my father's grave has been well tended, and I thank you."

Theadosia had taken on the duty, though she'd be hard put to give an excuse as to why. She'd convinced herself it was for the Duchess of Sutcliffe's sake. Still grieving, the woman visited her husband's grave for an hour every Sunday after services. When the weather permitted, she took lunch there too, her servants setting a table as fine as if she were dining at Windsor Castle with the king.

Poor lady.

Papa's keen gaze slid to Theadosia again, but he merely dipped his head and didn't reveal her secret.

Curious that. It was of no matter if the duke learned of it.

"I'd deem it an honor if you and your family, and Mr. Leadford, of course,"—that last seemed an afterthought on the duke's part—"would join us for dinner at Ridgewood Friday next."

Fingers crossed, she held her breath. She'd have time to finish her new gown by then. A couple of months ago, Papa had permitted Mama, Jessica, and Theadosia each four new gowns, as well as a new bonnet, gloves, and slippers. They'd never been afforded such luxuries before, and now that his grace had returned, she was even more grateful she'd not have to attend supper in one of her remade garments.

An intimate dinner with the Sutcliffes.

Oh, the marvel of it.

Her dearest friends, Nicolette Twistleton, twins Ophelia and Gabriella Breckensole, and their widowed cousin Everleigh Chatterton would demand all the details about the dinner when she and Jessica next met them for tea.

Please let Papa say yes. He must. *He must.*

She made her way to her father's side, but her dratted feet refused to budge an inch farther before she heard his reply.

"It would be our pleasure, Your Grace. I shall inform Marianne."

Papa's attention gravitated to the grand marble marker again.

Victor—that was, Sutcliffe—had found his father that awful night. He'd cut his body loose, and carried his sire into the house. Such was his anguish, afterward, he'd hacked the willow down and burned every last branch, even setting fire to the stump.

In the days following the duke's suicide, that topic had been on everyone's tongue except the Brentwoods'.

"If I may be of assistance in any way, do let me know. I am always available to counsel parishioners." Papa's offer was genuine. He truly cared for his flock and those that were suffering.

"There is one thing, if I may?" A wry smile bent the duke's mouth up on one side as he placed his hat atop his dark head. "I should very much appreciate you performing my wedding ceremony in August."

Theadosia flushed hot. Then cold. Then hot again.

Moisture flooded her eyes, blurring the grass she stared at.

He's betrothed.

That was why he'd returned. Of course he'd want to get married here. Why hadn't she considered such a thing? His homecoming wasn't because he'd missed Colchester at all. He'd probably leave straightaway after he exchanged vows too.

Swallowing gut-wrenching disappointment, she forced her feet to move. Stupid to have entertained fanciful hope all these years: a child's ridiculous fantasy. Daughters of rectors couldn't—shouldn't— yearn for passion and adventure. That was the drivel of romance novels. No, they married men of equal station. Staid, religious fellows with nice eyes and kind faces.

But not men who leered at bosoms.

"Indeed. Congratulations." Sincere excitement lit her father's voice. Except for Christmastide services, he adored nothing more than performing wedding ceremonies. "Do we know your future duchess?"

Did they?

Please God, not one of my friends.

No, the girls would've mentioned something as monumental, and there'd not been as much as a whisper about the Duke of Sutcliffe's upcoming nuptials.

An outsider then.

Likely some elegant, blue-blooded debutant with unblemished alabaster skin, petite feet, and a dowry so immense a team of dray horses couldn't pull the treasure.

Theadosia's dowry wouldn't fill a teapot. Or a teacup, for that matter.

She couldn't resist a last glance over her shoulder, and her gaze collided with Sutcliffe's.

"Perhaps." Another smile, this one humorless, hitched his grace's mouth up a notch. He seemed to speak directly at her.

"I confess, I don't know who she'll be yet."

3

The next afternoon, after suffering through a wretched head-pounding, stomach-churning morning thanks to his over-indulgence, Victor made his way to the sunroom.

The same gilded-framed portraits and paintings lined the walls, the same Aubusson rugs adorned the floors, and the same valuable trinkets and knickknacks topped the rosewood tables as he strode the wide corridor to the west wing.

Everything remained as it had been when he left, and yet nothing would ever be the same. He'd seen the very worst in himself as he tried to bury his grief and anger. Drinking, womanizing, and gaming—engaging in all the vices his sire had abstained from and denounced.

Rubbing his left brow with two finger pads, he closed his eyes for a moment. A niggling ache had settled there. Past experience had taught him the pain would remain with him for several hours. How many more hangovers must he endure before he forswore drunkenness?

How heartily disappointed Father would be. Mother too.

With justification, for until yesterday, Victor had intended to find the dowdiest, most biddable mousey miss to take to wife. And when he returned to London to resume his philandering lifestyle, he'd leave her at Ridgewood to keep Mama company. That plan hadn't altered, but knowing Father had taken his life instead of letting cancer steal it from him had made a difference in how he felt about his sire.

Not enough of a difference to make him want to stay at Ridgewood, though the knowledge stripped him of the excuse to carouse to excess anymore.

Partially.

Now a new fear taunted him. Grandfather had also died of cancer, as had an uncle. Was Victor the disease's next victim? Did that horror lurk in his future?

A smirk of self-reproach tipped his lips as he knocked softly on the doorframe of the sunroom's open door.

"Do you have a moment, Mother?"

Pulling her spectacles from her nose and laying aside the volume she'd been reading, she smiled a warm greeting and patted the settee.

"Victor, darling. Of course I do. What is it you need, dearest?"

Two years past her fifth decade, with only a few silvery strands amongst her ebony hair, his mother was a lovely woman. He'd inherited her hair and mouth, but it was his father's eyes that peered back at him in the mirror each morning.

His stomach tumbled.

Would he ever get the image of those bulging sightless orbs out of his mind?

He kissed her upturned cheek, the lightly

powdered flesh soft and unlined. Nudging her raggedy cat, Primrose, out of the way, he settled onto the ruby brocade cushion beside his mother. Now his dark maroon jacket would be covered with orange and white cat hair.

Primrose cracked open her one citrine eye and yawned, baring her needle-sharp fangs before lazily stretching and hopping onto the floor. In the most immodest display, she proceeded to groom herself.

Why ever had he thought to have the mangy beast delivered to Mother when he'd found it lying injured beside a barrel on London's wharf?

Because he knew his mother was lonely.

Her blue eyes brimming with happiness, she patted his cheek as she had when he was a small lad.

"I'm glad you're home, Victor."

She'd never complained about his neglect, which served to increase his guilt all the more.

Naturally, he'd written at least weekly and sent gifts too. His two sisters had visited regularly, their husbands and offspring in tow. Mother told him as much in her letters. But other than the dozen staff members who kept Ridgewood Court operating without a hitch, and her spoiled beyond redemption one-eyed cat, no one else resided in the house.

Thrice he'd directed the coach to be readied for the journey from London to Colchester. In the end, the grotesque image of his father's dangling body slowly spiraling 'round and 'round sent him in search of strong drink instead.

Damn him for a selfish arse; if it weren't for the stipulation in his father's will that he marry by his seven-and-twentieth birthday, or everything unentailed, including Ridgewood Court, transferred to his cousin, Victor mightn't have returned even now.

He'd never know why Father added that addendum only a few months before he died. At the reading of the will, Mother had been equally startled about the extra provision.

But she loved Ridgewood Court. It was here she'd come as a giddy new bride and here she'd given birth to her three children. And it was here that her husband, the man she'd adored for eight-and-twenty years, had taken his own life.

Did Mother know Father had cancer?

She would suffer no more loss or pain if Victor could prevent it. For certain she would not lose her home, which meant he had just over a month to locate a suitable bride. He'd chosen to return to Colchester, to his boyhood home, hoping there or somewhere in Essex, he could find a woman content to remain at Ridgewood while he resumed his life in London.

Small likelihood of that if he wanted an heir. But did he after all, given the cancer that ran in the family line? Even less possibility he'd be anywhere near as happy as his parents had been, for theirs had been a love match.

In fact, if he stood any chance of meeting his father's deadline, he would have to enlist Mother's help. He shouldn't have waited this long to come back to Ridgewood, but every time he considered returning home, the vision of his father's lifeless body stopped him.

Even now the image tormented him.

The corpse had been warm when Victor found him.

If only he'd been a few moments sooner he might have saved his father's life. But he hadn't known about the cancer either. Would watching his father die a slow, agonizingly painful death truly have been better?

Mother clasped Victor's hand and gave his fingers a tiny squeeze.

"Victor? What is it? You look troubled, and it's only your first day home."

"Mother, there's something about Father's death you might not know."

Her blank expression revealed what he suspected. She hadn't known either.

"He didn't just—" He paused and covered her hand with his. "Father had stomach cancer."

She gasped, pressing a palm to her throat as tears welled. Struggling for control, she withdrew a lacy scrap from her sleeve and dabbed at her eyes. At last, she collected herself and raised grief-ravaged eyes to his.

"I suspected he was ill, but when I questioned him, he said it was nothing to fret about. When and how did you find out?"

"Yesterday, at All Saint's Church. Theadosia Brentwood told me. She overheard her father some time ago and feared speaking of it. I'm glad she did. It was the not knowing why that ate away at me."

"Trust me, darling, I well understand that." She gave a tremulous, fragile smile. Sniffing, she touched the handkerchief to the corner of her eye again. "Cancer." She nodded, lips pressed tight. "Yes, he wouldn't have wanted to die that way, the way his uncle did. It was awful."

Hanging himself was so much better?

Victor shook off his morbid mental musings and forced a cheerful smile.

"I hope it's not an imposition, but while visiting Father's grave yesterday, I invited the Brentwoods and the new curate to dine with us next Friday."

Best not tell Mama he'd been a maudlin drunk when Thea came upon him.

Thea.

He'd nearly been struck dumb upon seeing her. Her soft brown eyes, the color of lightly burnt sugar— as sweet and warm too—had lit up in delight when she recognized him. An answering joy had peeled inside his soul as well.

By God, she'd grown into a beauty.

Even soused as he had been, he noticed the glow of her ivory skin, her finely arched brows, that pert pink rosebud mouth, and those jaunty reddish-blonde curls framing her oval face.

No timid mouse there.

She most definitely did not fit into his well thought out scheme of marrying and abandoning his bride.

Now where had that thought come from? It was ridiculous, surely.

"We've plenty of time to prepare. It's not an imposition at all. In fact, with your permission, I'd like to have a house party in a couple of weeks or so." Mama's eyes glittered, and she clapped her hands twice in excitement. "Oh, let's do have a ball too, Victor. That is if you're agreeable. It's been a long while since music and gaiety filled Ridgewood. Your sisters could come stay as well."

How could he deny her?

Relaxing against the back of the settee while hooking his ankle across his knee, he nodded.

"Yes, I think that's a grand idea. Do invite the Brentwoods, won't you?"

"All right darling, but I doubt they'll attend."

He stopped toying with the tapestry pillow. "Why?"

"I don't think you're aware, but the eldest Brentwood girl eloped a couple of years ago. With a traveling musician or acrobat or some such unpromising person." She waved her hand casually. "It caused quite a stir. You should be aware the reverend won't speak of her at all, nor will he permit others to. His daughters are rarely permitted social functions that aren't church related. He may not allow them to attend the house party or ball."

"That's awfully harsh, don't you think?"

It explained why Thea had been worried about being caught with him yesterday. It also dashed his excuse to hold her in his arms again while he waltzed her 'round the ballroom or terrace.

Mother rolled a shoulder. "He's a man of rigid

beliefs, and while I do not approve of his daughter's scandalous behavior, I think it wiser to be merciful and slow to judge. We don't always know what motivates someone to take extreme action."

Sorrow turned her mouth down.

Now she spoke of Father.

Even after all this time, she grieved for him. They'd been soulmates, and when Father died, a part of Mother had too. Little chance she'd marry again. Still . . . Mayhap he'd add a name or two to the guest list. Available gentlemen of a certain age of whom *he* approved. No rogues or rakes, no men of *his* ilk, for his Mother.

He hesitated a moment. Might as well crack on and ask for her help in acquiring a bride. It might help distract her. "I'm certain you recall I must wed in August, or the unentailed property transfers to Jeffery."

Jeffery was a decent chap, and yet it grated to think he'd inherit simply because Victor had dawdled too long in finding a duchess.

"I know, dear." A soft, understanding smile curved her mouth. "And I knew when you were ready, you'd come home and face that dragon. I honestly cannot fathom what possessed your father to add that stipulation."

Neither could Victor, unless it was to guarantee the duchy an heir. "We'll never know, but I hope you will be able to advise me in my search for a bride. You know more than I who the eligible young ladies are in the area, and you know what I require in a duchess."

He'd no doubt that whomever he selected, the chosen lady would eagerly agree to the match. What sensible woman would turn down becoming a duchess?

Expression contemplative, her attention focused on the gardens beyond the mullioned windows, she held her chin between her thumb and bent forefinger.

"What about love, my dear? I'd much rather you waited until you found someone you love."

Victor sighed and rubbed his fingertips across his forehead.

"I shan't have you lose your home because of my selfishness." He pressed his lips together. He'd cause her no more unhappiness. "I know you love

Ridgewood."

"Darling, I can live anywhere as long as my children visit. Your sisters invited me to live with them numerous times, but I've stayed at Ridgewood for you." Patting his hand, she offered a gentle smile. "To give you a reason to return and face your demons."

She'd stayed here alone when she could've been with one of her daughters and grandchildren? All the more reason he could not disappoint.

"And it's because of your generosity, Mother, that I cannot ignore the codicil."

"Victor, even the best of marriages endures many challenges, and I worry that without love . . ."

"I've considered that, but the most I can strive for at this late juncture is to find someone compatible. Father robbed me of the chance for love."

Just as well.

Not one to deceive himself, he knew there was scant risk of a shattered heart in a marriage of convenience. Mother was a far stronger person than he, because he wouldn't take the chance of loving someone with all his being as his parents had. He'd seen what that kind of affection had done to his mother. Seen her utter devastation. No, better to not have emotions involved, most particularly since he was rushing into the *blessed* event, and he too might perish from cancer.

Fine lines of concern fanning the corners of her loving eyes as she searched his face, his mother seemed to come to a decision. She inhaled deeply and clasped her hands.

"All right. Let's start with a guest list that includes all the eligible young women in Essex."

"All of them?" Precisely how many were there? "I was thinking of a half dozen of the most quiet and acquiescent—"

Her delighted laughter rang out.

"Oh, darling, no, no." Another trill of laughter filled the room. "You'd be utterly miserable with a biddable wife. Oh, my goodness no! You're too intense to tolerate a compliant, submissive duchess for long. She'd bore you within months, and I fear your eye would stray. That would be unfair to her, since I know too well you are a man who will demand fidelity from your duchess. No, I think a spirited girl who gives as good as she gets is a far better choice for you."

Hell and damnation.

She'd just thrown a huge hurdle in his plan, even if she was bloody right.

"To avoid hurt feelings, however, I shall invite all the unmarried ladies in Essex. Even the Nabity spinsters. Does that satisfy you?"

Her mouth trembled, and he grinned. Her good humor was contagious.

"Perhaps you ought to select those of childbearing age, unless you don't want more grandchildren?"

Could he really subject his children to the same sort of pain he'd endured if this new fear of cancer became a reality? And what if his children were susceptible to the demon disease?

What choice had he?

Let Jeffery inherit the duchy too? What good would that do? They shared a grandfather and their paternal grand uncle had died from cancer.

"I may not produce any offspring, you know."

"*La*, Victor Nathanial Horatio, don't say such a

wicked thing! The Sutcliffes have never forfeited in that department." She swatted his arm, and as she rose from the settee, she chuckled. "You must admit hosting a ball and inviting all the eligible women in the area so you might find a duchess is similar to the fairytale, Cendrillon, is it not?"

Victor also stood. He draped his arm around her shoulders and kissed the crown of her head.

"Except I'm no prince, and there won't be a magical happily-ever-after."

"Don't be too sure. I knew the moment I saw Sutcliffe I'd marry him, and he swore he fell in love with me during our first dance." Lost in her long-ago memory, a sad, fragile smile tipped her mouth. After a moment, she collected herself and patted his shoulder. "If you've anyone else you'd like to invite to the house party and ball besides the friends you already wrote to ask if they might visit, you can tell me their names later."

Yes, as well as the middling-aged banker Jerome DuBoise and the widower Major Rupert Marston. One gentleman or the other might possibly be the solution to Mother's loneliness.

"It's times like this I do wish I had a secretary. Primrose is going to help me, aren't you sweetums?" She bent and scooped the tabby into her arms. "Now you run along, dear. Get some fresh air. I have to speak with Cook about next week's menu, and I have a guest list to compile."

She did indeed know Victor well. Understood this talk of weddings and brides and balls exacted a toll he couldn't keep hidden.

"Thank you, Mother. I think I'll go for a walk before my ride. There's another dragon I need to face."

This one a massive, angry, fire-breathing demon he must conquer before it destroyed him.

If he was going to marry and stay at Ridgewood Court for any length of time, he must face the image tormenting him. After giving her another hug and scratching Primrose behind her scruffy ears, he strode to the door.

"Oh, Victor. We need to set a date for the ball. There's a full moon in three weeks. Is that too soon?" Mother had followed him to the doorway. "That way you have time left if you don't find your bride before then or on that night."

Her forced cheerfulness didn't fool him. She didn't approve, but because she loved him, she'd support his rash decision.

"Three weeks is fine." Feeling decidedly wicked, he winked. "In fact, why don't you put *Duke seeks Duchess* on the invitation. No better yet, *A dance will decide the Duke of Sutcliffe's duchess.*"

"You inherited your father's droll sense of humor, darling, but I think you may be onto something. Let me ponder on it." She waved her hand at him, indicating he should proceed her out the door. "Now shoo."

One lodestone's weight lifted from his shoulders, Victor left the house after asking Grover, the butler, to send word to the stables to have Acheron saddled.

Mother would indeed see that every eligible miss in all of Essex was invited to the ball. All he had to do was pick one to be his duchess. But how to determine the right one? Or rather, not the worst one?

What did he really want in a wife?

Biddable and bashful, or boisterous and bold?

A vixen or an angel?

Why couldn't she be a bit of both?

Thea's impish smile flashed to mind.

He'd tasted that sweet mouth yesterday. Sampled enough to make him want more. Crave more than settling for a marriage of convenience. *A marriage of necessity.*

But time was against him, and he'd been selfish long enough, and no force on God's Earth would prevent him from marrying in order for Mother to remain at Ridgewood.

Somehow, he didn't think Theadosia Brentwood was the type of woman to marry for station or convenience, more was the pity. He sighed. Else he'd end his search for a duchess before it began. It didn't matter that she was a commoner. He couldn't care less that she'd never left Colchester in her entire life and knew nothing of *haut ton* customs.

Or that the minx had lied most adeptly yesterday.

He'd seen the apology in her soft gaze, had noticed her silently pleading for him not to betray her.

Surely, if he offered for her, she'd be content to

remain here, near her family, and yet enjoy the privileges a duchess warranted while he returned to London. She didn't seem the demanding sort. But neither was she a timid, agreeable dowd. Not by a long way.

Even though he'd been in his cups, she'd piqued more than his interest. Theadosia Brentwood wasn't the type of woman a man left behind and forgot about while he caroused in London.

He hadn't missed Mr. Brentwood's hawkish regard either. The man was no simpleton, and Victor would vow the reverend guessed something more had transpired between Thea and him, but had chosen to keep quiet about the matter.

The fact that Thea had volunteered a sizable purse to pay for the chamber organ and new choir robes probably had a lot to do with the rector's silence. She'd looked so contrite after telling her tarradiddle. Victor would never humiliate her by disputing her claim; she'd made it to protect them both.

He couldn't remember the last time he'd anticipated anything as much as seeing Thea again.

Friday next couldn't arrive soon enough for him. Then, hopefully Pennington, Bainbridge, Westfall, and Sheffield—four of his closest cohorts—would attend the house party and ball. Dandridge and his bride too.

Almost like old times when the chaps had come up from university.

Almost . . .

He forced his feet to take the meandering path that led past the stables toward the dovecote. A trio of giant willows graced the meadow near the lake, their wispy branches rustling softly. No trace remained of the tree Victor had cut down and burned.

As nature does, she'd reclaimed the charred ground. Now lush grass covered the area, the verdant carpet scattered with the pinks and yellows of ragged robin, buttercups, red campion blossoms, and birds-foot trefoil.

The tightness in his chest lessened with each step until he stood where the willow had once towered. Closing his eyes, he filled his lungs to capacity then blew out a long breath of air. For the first time in over three years, he understood why his father had taken his life.

He'd wanted to be in charge of his own destiny, not at the whim of a ruthless disease.

Now Victor could let go of his pain and confusion. His anger too.

"I forgive you, Father," he murmured softly. "I cannot judge or blame you any longer. I never should've."

For if he faced the same circumstances, might he not do the same?

No. He wouldn't.

He'd choose to fight death until his last breath.

Peace engulfed Victor, and an even greater weight fell away, this time from his soul.

A turtledove cooed nearby. It probably sat on a nest in one of the willows.

He opened his eyes and smiled, for the first time truly glad to be home.

Through the ash copse beyond the field, a flash of color caught his attention. A group of women ambled along the lane leading to Colchester, and one wore a familiar straw bonnet bedecked with blue roses.

Thea.

In a trice, he dashed to the stables and mounted Acheron. Like an infatuated buck, he galloped the gelding around the lake to intercept the ladies where the woods paralleled the track before a sharp bend in the road.

As he emerged from the shadow of the trees, the women stopped chatting and glanced upward.

Reaching to doff his hat, he realized he'd been so consumed with thoughts of his father, he'd forgotten it. His gloves too. He bent slightly at the waist instead.

"Good afternoon, ladies."

He intended the greeting for them all, but his attention centered on the tallest woman dressed in a fetching cream and cerulean gown. The colors made her lips appear rosier and her eyes more chocolaty brown today. They also complemented her strawberry-blonde locks to perfection.

"Good afternoon, Your Grace." Surely Thea's smile was a trifle more exuberant and warm than politesse required. "I trust you enjoyed your walk home yester eve?"

Minx. She was taunting him.

"It was most . . . sobering."

Her eyes widened the merest bit, and he swore her mouth twitched at his jest.

Whisky wasn't addling his senses today, and he looked his fill.

She was even more impossibly exquisite. The sun filtering through the leaves overhead revealed a smattering of freckles across her nose and cheeks that he'd missed yesterday.

Too adorably perfect.

Absolutely the wrong sort of female to be his duchess. He'd not be able to leave a woman like her behind, only to visit her a couple of times a year. So why did he not go on his way?

"I'm sure you remember my friends and my sister." Thea saved him chagrin by rattling off their names in case he didn't. She lifted a gloved hand and indicated each young woman in turn. "Miss Jessica Brentwood, Miss Nicolette Twistleton, and Miss Ophelia and Miss Gabriella Breckensole."

As one, the other ladies dipped into graceful

curtsies.

"It's a pleasure to see you again, ladies."

He vaguely remembered the Breckensoles and Miss Twistleton, and Jessica Brentwood, naturally. She greatly resembled her sister, though her hair was blonder and her eyes bluish-green instead of rich, warm cocoa he could drown in.

Perhaps one of these very women might be his duchess in a few short weeks. He already had a strong inclination as to which one he favored. But she wasn't the wisest choice if he intended to stick to his well thought out scheme to find the perfect duchess: amendable, compliant, undemanding, polite, and easy to get on with.

Boring.

Blast him for a fool, but Mother was right.

Thea approached Acheron, a look of wonder upon her face. "Oh, he's beautiful. His coat has a silvery glint. I've never seen the color before."

Acheron flared his nostrils, taking in her scent. Then the shameless beast nudged her chest.

She patted his neck and giggled, a musical gurgle

that wasn't the least grating or squeaky, as feminine laughter often was.

"Aren't you the lovely one?" Thea edged to Acheron's other side. Her tone confidential, and low enough that only he could hear, she said, "Thank you for not exposing me yesterday. Please forgive my lies. I assure you, it's not a normal habit."

He bent to pat the horse's neck and whispered from the side of his mouth, "Anything for a damsel in distress."

Her eyes widened in pleased wonderment.

On impulse, he touched her cheek and whispered, "Permit me to call upon you tomorrow."

A shadow flitted across her radiant features, and she shook her head, casting an anxious glance in the direction of her sister and friends. "No. That's impossible. Papa doesn't permit me callers. It's too soon after your arrival home, in any event."

No callers? Did the reverend intend to make his daughters spinsters? Was this because of the elder sister dashing off with an unbefitting fellow?

Victor wasn't giving up that easily. Theadosia

Brentwood intrigued him as no woman ever had.

"Then walk with me. Meet me at the east end of Fielding's orchard, by Bower Pool at ten o'clock tomorrow morning?"

"All right." A pleased smile slanted her mouth, and her cheeks pinkened becomingly as she dropped her gaze, her focus once more on his horse.

Only with supreme effort did he subdue the ridiculous smile that threatened to split his face.

The other women remained unnaturally quiet. Any time his sisters had been in their friends' company, the chatting and tittering seldom ceased, and certainly never for more than a second or two.

Drawing his attention away from Thea petting and cooing to his horse whilst cramming down a wave of jealousy that the animal was permitted what he was not, Victor raised his head.

The foursome stared at him.

Their regard, curious and speculative, perhaps even sympathy-tinged, gave him pause.

Thea had told them about his upcoming nuptials.

She must've also told them he didn't have a bride

yet.

He could see it in their inquisitive gazes.

Except Jessica Brentwood. Her expression didn't reveal her thoughts. He'd be bound the Brentwood misses had become adept at hiding their feelings with a father as severe as the reverend.

The news that the Duke of Sutcliffe sought a bride by August would spread faster than a fire in dried hay. Maybe inviting all the available females of a marriageable age to a ball wasn't the wisest decision.

Blast, of course it wasn't, but he didn't have much choice now, did he?

He'd dilly-dallied too long to go about courting, wooing, and paying his addresses, and with time running short, this strategy was the best he could think of.

A derisive snort almost escaped him.

Only a duke would dare *this* idiocy.

He considered Thea's bent head again.

Why look any further?

Wheels rattling and hooves *clopping* alerted him to a conveyance's approach.

He felt Thea's gaze on his face as surely as if she ran her long fingers over his features. He met her pretty sable-lashed eyes, and in their depths, he spied pity too.

That was too much.

Pity most certainly was not what he wanted from Theadosia Brentwood. Feeling very much the callow youth, he tipped his head.

"I look forward to dinner next Friday, Misses Brentwood. Ladies it was a pleasure to see you again."

He'd held his tongue about the house-party and ball. They'd learn about it soon enough in any event. Given Mother's efficiency, invitations would be posted by Monday. At least she had something to look forward to, something to occupy her time.

Forcing himself to ride on and not look back to see if *she* watched his retreat took rugged self-control. He'd be unwise to show partiality to anyone yet. Particularly given the good reverend's reputation for propriety.

What would Mr. Brentwood do if he knew Thea had agreed to walk with Victor unchaperoned?

Tar and feather him? Lock him in irons? Excommunicate him?

As he veered Acheron toward Ridgewood's drive, he looked over his shoulder, unable to resist one last glimpse of Thea.

Instead, he encountered the reverend's formidable glower.

4

Four days later, Theadosia cast a casual but hurried glance behind her as she turned down the path leading to Bower Pool.

Good. No one was in sight, and she relaxed a trifle.

It had taken some doing to manage an hour's absence each day, but her parents encouraged benevolent visits and assumed she was about charitable tasks. Taking her basket along aided in the pretext. There was always an ill parishioner to take soup to, a lonely elderly widow to share a cup with, or errands to run in Colchester.

Jessica had lifted her fair brows the past couple of

days, but said nothing.

Theadosia might have to take her sister into her confidence but was reluctant to do so since Jessica would also suffer Papa's anger if he found out about her clandestine meetings.

Theadosia gave a small, wry shake of her head.

Look what she'd been reduced to.

Sneaking about to meet a man, much the same way Althea had.

Theadosia willingly risked Papa's wrath, for every minute with Victor became a cherished memory. Their friendship, her greatest treasure. To hope for more wasn't wise, and so she didn't allow herself that luxury. She took every moment she was gifted and refused to look too far into the future, because looming on the horizon was the knowledge he'd come home to wed.

Just as he had the two previous days they'd met, Victor waited for her, tossing rocks into the calm pool while lounging against a stone as tall as he.

She stopped to observe him for a few moments, tracing every plane of his handsome face, simply soaking in his masculine beauty. She could look at him forever. The high slash of his cheekbones, the noble length of his nose, his granite jaw, and his jet-black hair glistening in the morning sun.

He seemed eager to meet her each day too.

Could the illustrious Duke of Sutcliffe truly esteem a humble parson's daughter?

Did he enjoy their friendship as much as she?

Joy bubbled in her chest, and a soft happy noise escaped her.

A mama duck quacked a warning, and her brood of eight peeping ducklings followed her into deeper waters.

Victor turned as Theadosia approached, a ready, welcoming smile tipping his strong mouth. However, it was his seductive hooded eyes that never failed to make her stomach quiver, her blood quicken in her veins, and her breath to throttle up her throat.

My, but he was a splendid specimen of manhood.

Some woman was going to be very lucky.

If she hadn't already been half in love with him before he'd returned, she'd had fallen completely sugar bowl over bum for him now. It probably would only lead to heartache, but each time he asked her to meet him again, she'd agreed.

Though they dared spend but an hour together each day, they talked about most everything. Parting became more difficult each time she had to say farewell.

After church last Sunday, he'd lingered outside; she was certain he did so in order to speak with her, but Papa had sent her and Jessica directly home, in Mr. Leadford's company, no less.

The annoying man had blathered nonstop about his previous position, his hope to have his own parish soon, and then—the queerest thing, truly—said he'd intended to wed shortly.

He'd wasted no time in that regard.

Scarcely in Colchester a week and he had designs on some young woman?

Which poor maid had he chosen for that dubious honor?

Or mayhap he was enamored with a woman he'd left behind. Did the poor dear know of his roving eye?

Despite his genial smiles and pleasant countenance, something about Mr. Leadford reminded Theadosia of a serpent.

Straightening to his impressive height, Victor plucked a salmon-colored rose off the rock beside him. Lifting the bud to his nose, he ambled her way, all sinewy grace.

Could any other man sniff a flower and still appear so wholly masculine?

"Ridgewood's rose gardens are in full bloom, Thea. I wish you'd permit me to give you a tour before their blossoms fade."

From habit, she scanned the area, searching for anyone else. After confirming they were alone and offering an apologetic smile, she relaxed a touch more.

"You know I cannot unless Mama or Jessica accompanies me. Even then, we'd have to have a legitimate charitable excuse to call. Papa wouldn't approve of me visiting just so that you could show me your gardens."

"Then let me call at All Saints, and I'll speak to him—convince him I've only honorable intentions."

And exactly what were his intentions?

She longed to ask but also feared his answer. He'd never given the slightest hint he might consider her for his bride. Why would he, when at least a score of women of noble birth lived within an hour's drive of Ridgewood?

Naturally, he was expected to pick someone of his own station, to keep that patrician lineage pure.

Wasn't that the way of the world?

"It's too soon, Victor."

She doubted Papa would ever permit him to call. He disapproved of everything about the duke. She'd bite off her tongue before she told him that, however. "Since Althea eloped, he's become most protective."

He held the rose out. "Here. I picked this for you. It's my favorite color of rose. It makes me think of your hair."

"Thank you. It's lovely." She accepted the lush blossom and couldn't resist inhaling the sweet fragrance. "We only have pink and white wild roses at All Saint's, and they don't smell half so wonderful as this."

As had become their habit, they began walking the pond's edge. Clouds littered the sky, but the temperature had warmed these past couple of days, so she only wore her spencer. She tucked the rose into the vee of the jacket, where she'd remember to remove it and hide it in the basket before she reached home.

The sweet aroma wafted upward, and, every now and again, her chin brushed the silky petals. She'd press it between the folds of a heavy book for safekeeping, to take out and look at when the blue devils overcame her.

By deliberate design on her part, perhaps on his as well, they never discussed his upcoming marriage. He also never touched her, except to help her over a stone, and then he released her the moment she regained her balance.

Theadosia found herself wishing he wasn't such a gentleman.

Papa was wrong about Victor. So wrong.

He was the most chivalrous, considerate man she'd ever met.

"You've received the invitation to the ball?"

His question was casual, but the tenor of his voice held a more serious note.

"Yes, but Papa hasn't said whether we are permitted to attend."

Mama, at Theadosia's and Jessica's behest, promised to do her utmost to see that they were allowed to go.

She edged the basket higher.

"I brought lemonade and seedcake." She gave him a coy look. "It's the Nabity sisters' recipe. They brought a cake by yesterday."

His eyes lit up, and he motioned to a large moss-covered root beneath a trio of giant beech trees.

"Let me remove my coat, and we can sit on it."

A few moments later, they relaxed atop the fine fabric, nibbling the delicious cake and sipping lemonade straight from the bottle. Theadosia couldn't help but notice the biceps and other muscles straining at the fabric of his fine lawn shirt.

She also couldn't help but observe the strong column of his throat or his lips when he put the bottle to his mouth and drank the sweet beverage.

Closing her eyes, she tilted her face upward, enjoying the sunlight filtering through the gently rustling leaves.

This was bliss.

"Thea?"

How she loved hearing her pet name on his lips. The way he said it, the low burr rolling off his tongue sounded like an endearment.

"*Hmm?*"

"Why did you agree to meet me, and continue to do so when you know your father will disapprove and you risk punishment?"

His voice came from nearby. Very near, his breath warming her ear and sending the most delicious tremors from her neck to her belly.

Slowly, as if waking from a deep slumber, she opened her lids, her gaze tangling with his molten stare. He was so close, she could see the silver shards in his eyes and smell his clean, woodsy scent.

"Because you asked me to."

It was much more than that, but even as brash as she'd been to defy Papa, she wasn't about to confess her most private secrets to Victor.

He was a man of the world, she an inexperienced parson's daughter.

His lazy smile washed over her like warm, fragrant oil.

"And would you do anything I asked you to?"

He gave her a raffish wink and waggled his eyebrows.

She giggled, then notched her chin upward.

"Certainly not, sir. I'm a reverend's daughter, the model of modesty and decorum."

"If I weren't a selfish man, I'd not keep asking you to meet me." He flicked a bit of something off her shoulder. "You risk much, and it's wrong of me to put you in that position. If only I might go about things the proper way . . ."

"I know what I'm doing, Victor. There is truth in what you say, and when I think it's grown too risky, we'll have to stop. But for now, let's enjoy each other's company."

He'd marry soon, and no new bride—marriage of convenience or not—wanted her groom meeting with another woman.

He took her hand and turned it over, running his fingertips across the inside of her wrist.

"Do you know what I'm most afraid of?"

This strong, commanding man was afraid of something?

"No. Tell me."

Giving in to the urge to touch him, she leaned into his shoulder, enjoying his firmness pressed against her.

Staring across the pond, he drew in a lengthy breath. "Cancer. My father was the third person in his lineage to succumb to it. How can I be sure that I or my offspring won't be cursed with the disease too? Is it even fair for me to have children and subject them to that possibility?"

Angling her head, she searched his dear face.

"Victor, we are never sure of anything in this life, nor can we know why good people become ill and die while others who are wicked through-and-through live charmed lives." She rolled a shoulder as she slipped her fingers between his thick ones. "We either live our lives to the fullest while we can, or we allow fear to steal any chance of joy or happiness from us."

His eyes deepened to charcoal as he tipped her chin upward with a crooked finger.

"Thea, would you ever—?"

At that moment, two bony-legged boys, following a pair of spaniels, charged from the cover of the trees. When they spied Victor and her, the children skidded to a stop and gawked.

Drat and double drat.

She didn't know the lads, but that didn't mean they hadn't recognized her or the duke.

After elbowing each other and whispering back and forth, they bent into awkward bows.

"Yer Graces," the older fellow said.

Theadosia shook her head. "Oh, I'm not—"

Barking and yipping, their dogs shot off after a rabbit, and after a hasty salute, the boys followed suit.

One little chap's excited voice echoed back to her.

"Wait 'til Mum hears we saw the duke and duchess close enough to spit upon."

5

Smoothing a hand over the periwinkle satin covering her lap, Theadosia curled her toes into her new beaded slippers. Unfamiliar rebellion tickled her tongue, and it took supreme effort to school her countenance into a compliant expression.

Papa was simply being impossible.

Mulish and pig-headed.

And unfair. *So dashed unfair.*

On the opposite carriage seat, legs crossed, his hands folded and resting on his paunch belly, he gave Theadosia and Jessica his sternest look. The darkling scowl he leveled at the worst sort of sinners. A glare neither of them deserved.

Well, maybe Theadosia merited it, but Papa didn't know about the duke's kiss or the secret walks with him, nor would he ever, so he had no call to be severe and cross.

"You represent our household and All Saints Church tonight, my dears. I expect modest and decorous behavior from you both. You will only answer direct questions from his grace, and as briefly as possible." Sternness scored deep lines in his face and pleated the corners of his eyes. "Do I make myself clear, daughters?"

"Yes, Papa, but won't the duke think that discourteous of us?"

Theadosia dared challenge him, while Jessica nodded her head and gave her sister a puzzled sideways glance. It wasn't often that a Brentwood offspring argued with their sire.

Since coming upon them walking home that afternoon last week, he'd lectured them multiple times regarding the matter. He clearly did not approve of the duke, yet he couldn't afford to affront All Saint's most generous benefactor either.

He was being unfair to Victor. Not once had he attempted to kiss her again or even hold her hand. She'd been the one to hold his.

She felt far safer with him than the ponce at her side just now.

Mr. Leadford, staring out the window and seated on Thea's other side, no doubt by deliberate design, tipped his mouth upward at the exchange, as if privy to some great secret.

This past week, he'd been a constant, annoying presence. Pulling out her chair for meals—*every blasted meal*, offering to carry whatever she happened to be holding, and continually appearing when she was alone in the house or gardens.

Surely Papa wouldn't approve any more than he'd approve of her secret outings with Victor.

Three days ago, her father had entered the drawing room as she played the pianoforte and seen Mr. Leadford leaning far too close whilst pretending to study the music. Her skin had practically peeled itself from her flesh and scuttled under the bookshelf to hide.

Oddly, instead of objecting, Papa offered a

peculiar smile and left the room.

Worse though than that uncomfortable moment, was Mr. Leadford's touching her the past few days.

Far beyond the pale.

First a slight brushing of hands, then boldly skimming her waist or back. Yesterday, he'd *unintentionally* walked into her and bumped her behind with his groin.

If that had been an accident, she was a nun.

She'd nearly gone straight to Mama and complained.

Except he was wily, always pretending not to notice the contact or begging her forgiveness for his clumsiness. Every instance could be excused as inadvertent. He didn't fool her though. The more time she spent with him, the more she became convinced Mr. Leadford's pious façade hid a lecher's heart.

She'd even warned Jessica to avoid him and to never be alone with the curate.

If Papa thought to play matchmaker, he'd best rethink that notion. Day old porridge—make that moldy, maggoty gruel—ignited more enthusiasm in her than the curate.

Besides, another had captivated her heart, and she prayed his repeated invitations to walk together meant he found her equally as fascinating, though he'd said nothing of the sort.

Mama, sitting between James and Papa, gave Theadosia an understanding smile.

"Oscar, the girls have always been models of propriety."

As had Althea before her *descent into sin* as Papa called it.

"There's no reason to expect they will fall short tonight, and I do believe Theadosia is correct. If they aren't cordial, our hosts may take offense. Then All Saint's Church might suffer from the Sutcliffes displeasure." Her soft brogue and reassuring words lessened the tension within the vehicle a trifle.

Nonetheless, Theadosia couldn't dispel a peculiar sense of foreboding.

"There will be multiple chaperones present." Mama tucked her arm into the crook of Papa's elbow and gave him a cajoling smile. "I don't think we need to worry about impropriety on anyone's part."

Exactly. Victor had been the epitome of gallant behavior. So much so that she'd wanted to box his ears and demand he kiss her again.

Guilt plagued Theadosia for deceiving her parents, but the emotion paled in comparison to the love simmering in her heart. If she had to be creative and less than forthright in order to see Victor, so be it.

Just as Althea had her beau.

Except Victor wasn't Theadosia's suitor.

A small frown pulled her mouth downward before she caught herself and arranged her face into a neutral expression.

It shouldn't be like this.

Theadosia longed to be straightforward with her parents, but Papa especially made that impossible, and she wouldn't give up those precious times with Victor.

She wouldn't. Not yet, in any event. That time would come far too soon.

"His grace was perfectly respectable when he came upon us the other day," Jessica ventured before giving Theadosia a secretive sideways look.

And every day they'd met too.

Theadosia wanted to applaud her shy sister's boldness.

"So was the serpent in the Garden of Eden," Papa snapped. "Yet Eve gave into temptation, and look where that landed mankind."

Why was he in such ill humor these past few days?

Surely the chance encounter he'd come upon with them and the Duke of Sutcliffe hadn't caused this foul temper.

Gads, imagine how riled he'd be if he knew of her walks?

Theadosia had been excited to dine at Ridgewood Court, and now, Papa had all but ruined the event.

Must he always be so stuffy and severe?

Must he continuously anticipate the worst when it came to his children?

"Come now, why all the fuss?" James's ready grin flashed as he nudged Theadosia's slipper. He possessed Papa's sandy blond hair and square jaw, but also had Mama's eyes, which the ladies quite admired.

As she'd anticipated, when James had arrived, he'd been delighted to learn the duke was in residence.

"Pon my rep, Sutcliffe is the greatest of gentlemen. Don't listen to the gossip. I assure you it's embellished."

Mr. Leadford made a sound suspiciously like a snort, earning him an acerbic look from James.

"Father, you've no need to fret for my dear sisters, I assure you."

Theadosia bumped his foot back in thanks. The habit had started as young children when they disagreed with something their father said and wanted the other to know they stood with them, but didn't dare voice their thoughts.

In the Brentwood house, Papa's word was absolute, uncompromising law.

Papa made a disbelieving noise in the back of his throat. "The duke is in the market for a wife. By August, no less. Told me so himself." His thickening chin edged upward in self-importance. "He's asked me to perform the ceremony."

That truth dampened her spirits no small amount.

James's eyebrows shot to his thick hairline. "Zounds? Truly?"

"Yes, James, I was there when he said it."

Seeing Theadosia's confirming nod, her brother drummed his fingertips on his thigh.

"That's news to me. The *le beau monde* too." He chuckled and rubbed his chin. "I can well imagine the teeth-gnashing by the many damsels that missed their opportunity to become the next Duchess of Sutcliffe. Did he mention how he intends to acquire his bride, since he disdained to pick from those in London for the Season?"

Why, James was enjoying this, the scamp.

"No, he did not, and it's of no import to us." Papa very clearly did not find the situation amusing. "Your sisters are not amongst those under consideration."

Theadosia squelched her cry of protest.

Why not?

"And pray tell me why not?" Bless James for his boldness. "Thea and Jess are accomplished and beautiful, kind and intelligent. I daresay Sutcliffe should be ever so lucky as to marry one of them. I'd quite like to call him my brother-in-law."

James gave Theadosia a secret, naughty half-wink, and her heart skipped a beat.

He couldn't possibly know of her infatuation or the secret rendezvous.

She'd been so careful and had told no one.

Not even Jessica.

In fact, she never spoke of Victor to ensure no one suspected her *tendre*. A girlish fascination she ought to have outgrown, particularly since she'd neither seen nor heard from the duke those three plus years when he'd been gone.

Oh, she'd written to him a score of times, but the letters were never posted. In fact, she'd always burned them upon completion, never having the nerve to actually send them off.

Nevertheless, similar to an ember laying dormant, the moment she saw him again, the feeling sparked anew. She'd almost burst into flames when he'd kissed her, and the fire burned hotly still. It grew in intensity each time they met.

In fact, she could yet feel his firm mouth on hers if

she closed her eyes.

A proper young woman would've been appalled when Victor kissed her. Would've promptly left and reported the offense. Perhaps even slapped his face. But she'd wanted that scrumptious kiss, wanted more of them even now.

Papa settled farther into the corner of the carriage.

"Theadosia and Jessica are simple country lasses, James—*he means unsophisticated and ignorant*—destined to marry men of the cloth."

And there it was.

What Theadosia had suspected for some time now. Unaccustomed anger toward him and Althea welled up within her.

Jessica slipped her hand into Theadosia's and gave her fingers a squeeze.

A silent rebellion.

She'd no more interest in marrying a man of the cloth than Theadosia did. No more than Althea had, but had her actions condemned her sisters to lives neither wanted?

Was Theadosia to have no say at all about whom

she married?

Jessica either?

Mr. Leadford perked up upon hearing Papa's declaration and drew his attention from the passing scenery to strip Theadosia bare with his oily gaze again.

Why did no one notice, save she?

He met Papa's eyes for a second before glancing at Theadosia and giving her an eerie half-smile. "Fancy clothes and titles can turn a young woman's head, but the Good Book says God is not a respecter of persons, and neither should we be."

"And it also says to give honor to whom honor is due," Theadosia said.

Pompous twit.

Who did he think he was, lecturing her? If she didn't know otherwise, she'd think his look possessive.

Yes, something went on here.

She scooted closer to Jessica, not that the cramped carriage allowed her to put much distance between herself and Mr. Leadford.

Every time the vehicle hit a bump, he pressed his

thigh into hers.

At first Theadosia believed it unintended, but after the third time, given his previous lewd behavior, she changed her mind. The unscrupulous man took advantage of the jostling to touch her, the *roué*.

His accommodations might be on the other side of the parish, but she'd begun putting a chair beneath her bedchamber door handle before retiring.

"Your sisters are not accustomed to suave rakehells' charms, James," Papa said.

Good Lord, why wouldn't Papa let the matter go?

"James, I expect you and your mother to keep a sharp eye on the girls tonight. I covet your help as well, Hector."

Hector? Not Mr. Leadford?

Papa had *never* addressed the other curates by their given names.

Mama rolled her eyes, her impatience with the subject at an end.

The queer flopping in Theadosia's belly had as much to do with her growing suspicion as Mr. Leadford's sly touches.

"As you wish, sir." Mr. Leadford gave a deferential nod, his submissiveness as phony as Dowager Downing's ill-fitting false teeth.

Toady. Cur. Debauchee.

Straightening his cuff, Papa nodded his satisfaction. "One cannot be too cautious when dealing with aristocrats."

For heaven's sake, he made the Duke of Sutcliffe sound like Satan's offspring, and yet he remained oblivious to the evil sitting a few feet away.

Victor had never regarded her in the lascivious manner Mr. Leadford did.

The carriage lurched once more, and Theadosia almost yelped when his fingers brushed her waist.

Eyes narrowed, she clamped her jaw.

So help her, if Mr. Leadford touched her one more time, curate or not, she'd scream and pinch his roving hand.

James shook his head, concern replacing his earlier humor. "You don't know Sutcliffe as I do. There's no need to worry. He's a decent chap through and through."

Dear James exaggerated, but his loyalty to the duke was sweet.

Even in Colchester one heard tattle of the Duke's exploits. She supposed he was no different than any other young blood in London. Privilege, position, wealth, and power were taken for granted by those who possessed them, and one didn't have to be terribly astute to know the *haut ton* had a separate set of rules for the behavior of those welcomed into their elite ranks.

And still, knowing full well his reputation, she'd freely agreed to see him. Had eagerly done so—would continue to.

James bumped her foot again and waggled his eyebrows as if to say, "Don't worry."

Lucky James.

He could leave after Sunday service and likely wouldn't find his way home for another month. There'd be no one to champion her and Jessica. His position as a barrister saved him from Papa's interference in his life. He had greeted James's choice to refuse to enter the ministry with his usual bluster.

But in the end, her brother had prevailed and was permitted to pursue his dream.

Theadosia wouldn't be allowed the same license.

Women rarely were.

A few minutes later saw them ushered into Ridgewood Court's formal drawing room. Once before, after the former duke died, the Brentwoods had sat upon these sage and gold brocade chairs and settees. They'd called to pay their respects and for Papa to confer with her grace about the funeral arrangements.

Confident in her second-best new gown of palest blue-lavender, Theadosia covertly searched the room for Victor.

He wasn't there.

The two days since she'd seen him had crawled along, inch by endless inch, and worry he might not join them after-all stole her earlier joy.

Wearing a stunning wine-colored gown edged in gold and black with matching rubies at her throat and ears, the duchess stopped petting a bedraggled, one-eyed cat and greeted them with a warm smile.

"I'm so delighted you accepted Sutcliffe's invitation. Now that he's home, we intend to entertain more often. I'm sure you've received the invitation to the house party and ball by now."

"Indeed, Your Grace," Mama affirmed. "It arrived two days ago."

Theadosia exchanged glances with Jessica. Had Mama convinced Papa to permit them to attend?

"You must all promise to come. It's to be a very special occasion. Why, there's never been anything quite like it in all of Essex. I shan't take no for an answer." The duchess looked directly at Theadosia and smiled again.

She'd forgotten how tall the duchess was. It made her feel less conspicuous and awkward.

"Of course we shall." Mama agreed before Papa had an opportunity to contrive an excuse not to. "I, for one, cannot wait. A fairytale masquerade ball sounds so fascinating."

On occasion, Mama's Scottish temper flared as red as her hair. The determined set of her chin brooked no argument. They would attend the house party and ball, except, unlike the other guests, they'd return home to sleep, their journey lit by the full moon. Unless the weather continued to be exceptionally cool, as the summer had been so far, and clouds filled the sky.

The butler entered bearing a tray with a sherry decanter and glasses.

"Shall I pour, Your Grace?"

"Yes, please, Grover." Her smile brightened even more as she glanced toward the entrance. "Ah, there you are, Sutcliffe."

Theadosia slowly turned, bracing herself for the onslaught of emotion and sensation that beset her each time she saw Victor. Her breath stalled nonetheless. Formal togs suited him well. The truth was, he could wear rags, and she'd react the same.

He directed one of his dazzling smiles at her; the one that made her pulse dance and her stomach tumble, and, uncaring who witnessed the exchange, she smiled back, letting the upward arc of her mouth reveal how delighted she was to see him.

In short order, Theadosia found herself seated on a

settee between him and Mr. Leadford, each holding a glass of sherry. Rather, she'd unwisely sat upon the settee to pet the bedraggled cat, and Mr. Leadford had promptly plopped down on the other cushion.

Much like a large raptor hunting its prey, he'd swooped in to claim his quarry.

She'd nearly fallen off her seat when Sutcliffe lifted the cat, and after setting the miffed feline on the floor, took its place.

He'd sport orange and white hairs on his behind when he stood.

Theadosia eyed him from the corner of her eye. She didn't quite know what to think.

He almost acted . . . jealous.

Preposterous notion. Delicious, wonderfully absurd idea.

Jessica and James stood beside the fireplace, entirely too amused expressions on their faces as they looked on. She gave them a narrowed-eyed, stop-being-great-loobies-look.

Her parents chatted with the duchess, but Papa's frequent unsettling glances in Theadosia's direction had her shoulders cramping with tension.

Something was off.

She didn't know what, but every instinct she possessed screeched a warning.

Ever since Mr. Leadford's arrival, Papa hadn't been himself. Always serious and not ever inclined to silliness, he'd become short-tempered, impatient, and critical as well.

Even Mama had raised her brow askance several times.

Mr. Leadford, his countenance all congenial interest, rested his forearm on the arm of the settee and cocked his head.

"How does your search for a bride go, Your Grace?"

6

His question bordered on impertinent, but for the life of her, Theadosia couldn't prevent herself from glancing at Sutcliffe.

How *did* his search go?

Bloody, horridly awful, she hoped.

They'd not discussed that subject during their walks. She hadn't wanted to know if he'd chosen a bride yet. Not likely, since he'd only been home a short while, but not impossible either.

She deciphered nothing from his closed expression. So very different than the man in the cemetery with his easy smile and twinkling eyes, or the relaxed companion who'd strolled beside her by the lake.

Sutcliffe shifted his attention to her for a moment, and something fascinating flashed in those cool grey depths. Just as quickly, the gleam vanished, and he took a sip of sherry.

"It *goes*."

He crossed his legs, and, resting a long arm across the settee's carved back, dismissed Mr. Leadford.

"Miss Brentwood, do you and your sister ride? Our horseflesh isn't getting enough exercise, and I am hopeful you might be willing to take a horse out a couple of times a week."

As it had in the cemetery and that day they'd shared seedcake, the world shrank until it was just the two of them.

What was it about this man that stirred her very soul?

His mouth ticked up on one side. "Do you ride?"

What had he asked her?

Oh, yes, did she ride?

"I do, but not terribly well. I'd appreciate the opportunity to practice."

If Papa could be persuaded to agree.

About as much of a chance of that as the Regent serving them dinner wearing a pink wig. No wonder Althea had revolted under their father's firm hand or that James had escaped to London rather than follow in their father's footsteps. Mutinous stirrings plagued Theadosia also, and if Papa continued down this track of oppressiveness, Jessica might well rebel too.

"Surely your stable hands are capable of exercising your cattle." Mr. Leadford did not ride. In fact, from what she'd observed, horses frightened him. "Miss Brentwood admits she doesn't ride well. I'm sure she's only being polite by agreeing. A gentleman wouldn't impose—"

"No, Mr. Leadford, I am not simply being polite." The infuriating man. How dare he? "Please do not speak on my behalf. Unlike you, I quite like horses, and it is no imposition to take a horse out now and again. In fact, I would consider it a refreshing change of pace."

Enough was enough.

She'd risk Papa's ire by speaking her mind. He must be apprised of Mr. Leadford's behavior: his galling forwardness and impudence. He, too, was a representative of All Saint's Church and, since Sutcliffe's entrance this evening, had been nothing but insolent.

Leveling Mr. Leadford a scathing scowl that would have wilted a man with any degree of common sense, Victor shrugged. With an offhand flick of his fingers he answered the curate.

"I am short-staffed at present, and we've not had many visitors of late to take advantage of our stables. Guests will be arriving for our house party in a fortnight, but the horses need to stretch their legs before then."

"I cannot imagine why you must marry so soon, especially since you haven't even selected a bride. A bit of a conundrum and no small degree of awkwardness, I should say."

Is he an utterly ill-bred buffoon?

His abrupt change in subject earned him a cocked brow from Sutcliffe.

No doubt the smile Leadford bestowed upon her was meant to flatter, but all it did was turn her stomach.

"*I* could only wed a woman who'd captured my regard." His calculating gaze trailed over her, and she barely resisted the urge to fold her arms over her breasts. "Then *I* would court her for a respectable period before our wedding, to prevent gossip or speculation."

The bounder mocked Victor whilst attempting to stake claim to her.

If they'd been alone, she'd have unleashed her temper and tongue.

"Some of us aren't allowed such luxury." Sutcliffe's dry as chalk response only served to confuse Mr. Leadford.

"Since when is love a luxury?" Mr. Leadford asked.

"When you hold a title, circumstances compel decisions, not emotions." Even to Theadosia's ears Victor's clipped response resonated with aloofness.

Inexplicable disappointment dampened her mood.

Again, Sutcliffe's gaze found hers. This time, his held a trifle longer, and something invisible passed between them, almost as if he sent her a silent message.

Why must he marry in such haste? He'd never told her.

There must be a compelling motive. He didn't seem a man of impetuous whims.

"I'm sure the Duke has his reasons, and in truth, they aren't any of our business, are they?" Theadosia arched a condemning brow at Mr. Leadford as she lifted her glass and took a drink.

A man of God should be more discreet and considerate.

The butler entered, thankfully interrupting the stilted silence on the settee. "Dinner is served, Your Grace."

"Excellent. Shall we pass through?" The duchess accepted Father's extended elbow.

Victor rose and, since Mama was the highest-ranking female, offered her his arm. The look he slid Theadosia suggested he'd rather have escorted her, and her heart leapt at the secret glance that passed between them.

"Mrs. Brentwood, I wonder if I might persuade you to make that delicious marmalade I remember so well?" Victor said. "I've not had the like in years. I even brought oranges home, hoping you'd indulge me."

A flush of pleasure tinted Mama's cheeks. "I would deem it an honor, but I must confess Theadosia's surpasses mine these days."

He looked over his shoulder, and pleasant warmth swathed Theadosia again. "Then might I persuade you, Miss Brentwood?"

Oh, he could persuade her to do a whole lot more with those sultry glances.

"Of course. Just have the fruit delivered to the parsonage. I can make it next week." Did she sound too eager? "I'd planned on making preserves anyway."

There, that made her willingness a little less obvious.

James's mouth hitched upward an inch before he schooled his features.

Drat and blast.

He knew. Or at least he suspected.

Mr. Leadford, the uncouth boor, offered her his elbow. Did the man know nothing of protocol? As the eldest daughter, she was to have gone in with her brother. James outranked him, but unless she wanted to appear intolerably rude, she must accept the curate's proffered arm.

A slight grimace pulled her generally jovial brother's brows together as he escorted Jessica past. She rose up on her toes and whispered something in his ear, and he nodded, then shrugged.

Theadosia barely rested the tips of her fingers atop Mr. Leadford's arm as he brought up the rear. She'd prefer touching a dead rat. Her revulsion would definitely be less.

Mama and Papa had taken seats to the right and left of Victor, and a footman was in the process of refilling Papa's wine glass. He'd also indulged in two sherries before dinner. Most unusual behavior. He rarely drank more than one glass of spirits during an entire meal.

James had claimed his rightful position beside Mama, and Jessica sat opposite him.

Which meant Theadosia was spared Mr. Leadford's presence next to her for the meal, for only two chairs remained.

On opposite sides of the table.

Praise God and hallelujah.

His ignorance proved her saving grace. Otherwise, she'd be sitting where Jessica sat, and have to endure his intolerable presence with a forced smile whilst trying to keep down her meal.

Mouth turned down, his annoyance as obvious as the red pimply thing on the end of his chin, his attention wavered between the empty chairs. He paused before sluggishly dragging Theadosia's chair out.

"I beg your pardon, Miss Jessica. I believe I've committed a *faux pas* and usurped your brother's right to escort your sister to the table. Please sit here, and Miss Brentwood can take her rightful place."

Beside him.

The smile he gave Jessica might've won over another, but she wasn't having any of it.

She might be timid, but her insight and

intelligence were razor sharp. As regally as if she were the grand hostess this evening, she unfolded her serviette.

"I do thank you, but since we are already seated, and I should not like the soup to grow cold, let's remain as we are. What say you, Your Grace?"

She looked to the duchess for confirmation.

Another bravo for Jessica tonight. Two times in one evening she'd voiced her opinion. Perhaps she was outgrowing her bashfulness.

"Indeed, Miss Jessica. I do so loathe cold white soup."

The duchess lifted her spoon, and pointedly looked to the other vacant chair.

"Of course, Ma'am," Leadford mumbled, the tips of his ears tinted red as he held the chair out for Theadosia.

To Theadosia's credit, she suppressed her jubilant smile as she slid onto the seat but couldn't resist a secret wink in Jessica's direction.

Victor saw it and lifted his wine glass an inch in a silent salute.

"Spared by a hair, sister dearest," James whispered in her ear.

The meal proceeded pleasantly for several minutes. Theadosia's attention seemed to have developed a mind of its own and kept straying to the head of the table. More than once she caught Victor's eye, and something glowed there that fanned the fire burning within her ever hotter.

She'd better take care lest Papa notice too.

He'd emptied his wine glass twice already, and this was only the third course.

Mama had noticed too, and a little furrow wrinkled her forehead.

"Miss Brentwood," her grace touched the back of Theadosia's hand. "I've never thanked you for attending my late husband's grave."

Theadosia swung her focus to the duchess.

How did she know?

The duchess must've seen the question in Theadosia's expression.

"I mentioned it to Mrs. Brentwood after church one Sunday. She told me it was you who saw to the grave's care."

Cutting her mother a swift glance, Theadosia nodded, offering a closed mouth smile and lifting a shoulder.

"It was no bother. Truly."

She far preferred tending the graves and gardens than the myriad of indoor chores that always needed doing.

"I'd like to thank you by inviting you to tea next Wednesday. Just you and me." The duchess took a sip of wine, her regard on Victor. "Perhaps you would consider helping me with the final plans for the ball as well? I truly could use an assistant. There are so many details to oversee, and Sutcliffe is quite useless when it comes to these sorts of things. He suggested I ask you."

He had?

Theadosia didn't need a mirror to tell her bright color tinted her cheeks. Had she been so obvious that even his mother noticed her frequent glances toward her son?

"I would deem it an honor, ma'am."

If Papa permitted it.

Theadosia would appeal to Mama. If anyone could make Papa agree, it was her mother.

Mr. Leadford narrowed his eyes, and he stabbed a piece of pheasant quite viciously. "Is the ball to be a celebration of the duke's upcoming nuptials?"

As sometimes happens during social gatherings, all conversations paused at the same moment and his question rang out loudly.

Silence, awkward and heavy, filled the room.

Her grace turned a frigid stare on him, whilst delivering a polite set down. "The ball is a celebration of my son returning home after an extended absence."

Swallowing mortification for Victor, Theadosia kicked Mr. Leadford under the table.

Hard.

Twice.

He grunted, harsh lines scoring his face and his eyes accusing her.

"I beg your pardon. Muscle spasms." She forked a carrot and blinked in exaggerated innocence. "I've had them since childhood. Just one of my *many* embarrassing faults."

Not entirely an untruth. She'd had a few instances of her leg muscles jerking before her eighth birthday but not one since. As for her faults, until recently when she'd taken up telling tarradiddles, Papa had seen to it she'd make the ideal parson's wife.

All the more reason to start engaging in further mischief.

Her grace's mouth trembled, and Theadosia thought perhaps approval sparkled in her pretty eyes.

With a flick of his long fingers, Victor indicated he wanted more wine. Once the glass had been filled, he lifted it and looked 'round the table, almost in a challenge.

His focus returned to her for a fleeting second before he leveled Mr. Leadford a bored stare.

"Truth to tell, if all goes well, I intend to select my duchess at the ball."

He did?

Without knowing the woman in advance?

Why would he do such a thing? He'd not mentioned anything of the sort to her.

This was real life, not a fanciful fairytale where happily-ever-afters were guaranteed.

She'd no right to feel vexed or deceived, and yet she did.

Was marriage truly so unimportant to him, just a duty he had to fulfill? His response to Mr. Leadford earlier hinted at that very thing, but she'd not have believed Victor so callous and uncaring. Then again, he'd left his mother alone for years.

True, but he'd also wept over his father's grave.

Did his fear of cancer have anything to do with his cold-hearted decision?

Tears burned behind her lids, and Theadosia sank her gaze to her plate.

How could she attend the ball and stand by silently, watching him select his duchess?

She willed the wetness to cease. By George, she would not cry and give herself away. Later, when she was alone, she could sob into her pillow and berate herself for a nincompoop. But for now, she marshaled her composure and put on a brave face.

Nonetheless, she couldn't possibly help his mother

plan the dance. Now wasn't the time to cry off, however. A note tomorrow would suffice.

"Tut, Sutcliffe, you jest. I've said so often, but it's true. You have your father's dry humor." His mother shook her intricately coiffed head, her earrings swaying with the motion. "The ball is merely to help you become reacquainted with everyone since you've been away for so long."

"We're to celebrate a union soon as well," Papa said.

Mouth parted in astonishment for the second time in as many minutes, Theadosia abruptly turned her head in his direction. His speech wasn't slurred, but his lopsided smile bespoke drunkenness, a trait he railed against from the pulpit on a regular basis.

He wouldn't meet her eyes, but instead drained his glass once more. Something in his countenance sent an alarm streaking down her spine.

No. He wouldn't. Not like this.

Not without telling her first. Not without asking if she was agreeable to the match.

"Brentwood, you are betrothed?" Victor's mouth

curved into a congratulatory grin and he raised his glass to James. "I wish you happy."

A mixture of concern and bewilderment puckering his usual jovial features, James shook his head.

"No, Sutcliffe, I am not. And to my knowledge, neither are my sisters."

He gave their father a hard, relentless stare.

A perplexed scowl pulled Victor's ebony brows together low over the bridge of his nose.

Mama, her posture as stiff as the table their food sat upon, very carefully laid down her fork and narrowed her eyes to mere slits. Sparks fairly flew from her accusing gaze.

"Whatever are you talking about, Oscar? Have you made an arrangement without speaking to me first? When we agreed you'd never do any such thing again?"

"I am her father." Papa seized his glass once more, blinking in puzzlement when he realized it was empty. He held it up, tipping it back and forth to indicate he wanted it refilled. "It is my right."

Her parents didn't squabble in public, and a blush

of mortification heated Theadosia from neck to hairline. Jessica's flushed face revealed she was likewise as discomfited.

Never had Theadosia been so embarrassed.

Never so utterly terrified. Or angry.

A footman dutifully refilled Papa's glass after receiving the slightest nod from Victor.

"We'll discuss this at home." Mama's tightened mouth revealed her displeasure, but she wouldn't argue in front of the Sutcliffes. Once they were home, however, she'd ring her husband a proper peal.

He swallowed, and after casting Mr. Leadford a harried glance, wiped his mouth with his serviette. He lifted his glass high.

"Please join me in a toast to celebrate Theadosia's upcoming betrothal to Mr. Leadford."

"No! Papa, no. You cannot do this to her. You cannot be so uncaring."

Theadosia barely heard Jessica's cries, for the room spun 'round and 'round.

"No . . ."

She struggled to her feet, knocking her glass of

wine over in the process.

The crimson spread across the white tablecloth.

Like my lacerated heart.

She couldn't look at Victor. Couldn't bear to see the pity or accusation in his glance.

"I . . . I need . . ."

I shall not marry that vile toad. I shan't. I shan't.

She touched her forehead, surprised to find the skin cool and clammy. The spinning increased, faster and faster. She stumbled again, banging into the table.

"She's going to swoon." The duchess jumped up and wrapped an arm around Theadosia's shoulder. "Sutcliffe!"

Theadosia couldn't hear through the whooshing in her ears. Everything became muffled, and everyone moved sluggishly. She tried to find Victor, but her vision had gone black.

"I shan't marry him." Hands extended before her, she shook her head, trying to clear her vision and hearing. "I shan't. I sha—"

"Thea!" Familiar arms, strong and sturdy, encircled her an instant before oblivion descended.

7

Torn between anger and frustration, and after having stayed up the entire night, Victor approached the parish's front gate. Though not quite nine o'clock, too early for a social call, he would wait no longer to approach Reverend Brentwood with a unique proposition.

He intended to ask for Thea's hand in marriage, and dower Jessica too.

Only a cod's head would pass up such a generous offer. If that didn't prove incentive enough, he'd keep enhancing his proposition until Brentwood agreed.

No official betrothal announcement had been made yet, no banns read, so Leadford couldn't claim breach of promise. Even if he tried, Victor would pay him off. He'd do anything to remove the wretch from Colchester and from Thea's life.

From her traumatic reaction last evening, she clearly had no notion her father had arranged a match with the curate.

Such anger had engulfed Victor toward the reverend for her public humiliation. What kind of father sprang something of that importance on his daughter during a dinner party? Given the smug satisfaction on Leadford's face, he'd known in advance and had enjoyed Theadosia's mortification.

Whilst sitting beside her on the settee last night, Victor hadn't missed her shudders of repulsion when Leadford pressed near. She couldn't stand the man.

Under no circumstances could she be forced to marry and bed that maggot.

Glancing around, Victor shifted the crate of oranges and gave the door a sharp rap.

The promised marmalade provided him the perfect excuse to call. Not that he really needed one. His position afforded him many privileges, and in this instance, he didn't hesitate to take advantage. He should have done so earlier, but out of consideration for Theadosia and her worry about his reception, he'd yielded to her wishes.

A quaint white arched gate covered in untamed white and pink roses stood ajar at the side of the house. Beyond the flagstone footpath visible through the opening, neat vegetable and flowerbeds basked in the morning sunlight. Chickens clucked, and a rooster crowed somewhere beyond the old, weathered, dry stone wall surrounding the grounds.

A flash of pink and green chintz appeared momentarily on a stone bench only partially visible from where he stood.

Thea?

He knocked again, hoping to avoid seeing her until he'd spoken to her father. Victor wanted to tell her himself of the change in plans for her future. Surely, if she must submit to an arranged marriage, she'd be more amendable to wedding a duke instead of Leadford.

After all, she at least knew Victor, and from that

stirring kiss they'd shared, she wasn't unaffected by him. Perhaps sexual attraction wasn't the best foundation to build a marriage upon, but it was better than him proposing to a stranger or her marrying a lecherous rotter.

Victor had seen Leadford's kind before. London teemed with that sort of vermin.

A man whose public façade hid an evil side. He hadn't missed Leadford's attempted peeks down Thea's bodice or the cawker's brushing against her. It had been all Victor could do not to pick the degenerate up by the scruff of his neck and shake him until his nice teeth rattled.

From his turned down mouth, James had noticed too.

Where was he, anyway?

Still abed? Not typical of him. More likely, he'd gone out for a ride as Victor and James had done as young men home from university.

Victor could use an ally in his quest, and given James's disapproval last night, Victor felt confident his long-time friend would support his suit.

He'd raised his hand to knock for the third time when Miss Jessica opened the door.

"Good morning, Your Grace. To what do we owe this honor?" Her gaze dropped to the oranges. "Oh, that's right. Thea is to make you marmalade."

A shadow darkened her pretty features, and lips pressed into a thin ribbon, she looked behind him. "She's in the garden."

"How is she?" he asked. "I know she suffered quite a shock last evening."

He'd been the one to carry Thea to the parlor, and he'd paced behind the settee while smelling salts were fetched. When her lashes fluttered open, it was his eyes she first met, and the despair glinting in those velvety depths bludgeoned him like a mule kick to the gut.

She'd silently pleaded with him, mouthing, "Help me."

In that instant, he was determined to do whatever was necessary to save her from Leadford.

"She's . . . adjusting to the news." After another glance toward the garden, Jessica shut the door. "Shall I fetch her for you?"

"Later. I'd like to speak to the reverend first. Is he home?"

Victor set the oranges down before passing her his hat and gloves.

Expression shuttered, she nodded as she set them on the entry table.

"Please have a seat, and I'll let Papa know you're here."

Rarely had Victor been inside the parsonage, even when he and James had spent a great deal of time together as youths. It remained much the same as he remembered.

Uncustomary nerves caused his palms to sweat and his stomach to clench.

He wouldn't have believed asking for a woman's hand would unsettle him this much. Wasn't that what he'd intended to do anyway? The only difference was, he was doing so before the ball rather than after.

Yes, but Thea wasn't just any woman, and the outcome of his conversation with Reverend Brentwood mattered far more than it ought to. As much for Victor as Thea.

"Sir? Papa will see you in his study." Jessica's countenance revealed nothing. "I'll let Thea know you are here as well."

"Thank you."

Victor followed her down the parish's time-worn corridor. If memory served, the building was nearly two hundred years old. Everywhere he glanced, evidence of decades of wear met his perusal.

Jessica stopped outside a slightly off kilter open door.

"Papa, the Duke of Sutcliffe."

Once inside the smallish, rather stuffy room, Victor took it upon himself to close the door.

"Thank you for seeing me without prior notice."

Mr. Brentwood cut an unreadable look at the closed door before waving his hand to one of two cracked leather chairs angled before his desk. Elbows resting atop the ink-stained surface, the rector cupped one hand over the other.

Was it Victor's imagination, or was Mr. Brentwood's calm demeanor meant to conceal the edginess his shifting gaze, taut jaw, and stiff shoulders couldn't hide?

Through the window behind the reverend, Victor glimpsed Jessica speaking to Thea. Both women turned toward the house, and even from where he sat, Victor could see the dark circles beneath Thea's red-rimmed eyes.

Shoulders squared, she held her head high, brave and unflinching.

Such admiration welled within his chest, he couldn't breathe for a moment.

By God, he'd save her from the fate her father planned for her, even if he had to abduct her.

Victor sank onto the chair, and the old leather crackled in protest.

"What can I do for you, Your Grace?" Mr. Brentwood's voice held the same chill his gaze did.

Might as well get straight to it.

Taking a bracing breath, Victor tore his glance from the vision of loveliness staring at the parsonage.

"I'm here to ask for Miss Theadosia's hand in marriage. I have a special license and would like the ceremony to take place immediately."

The rector acted neither surprised nor shocked. Instead he leaned back in his equally worn chair and pursed his lips.

"A special license? With the bride's name blank? How did you manage that?"

Definite censure there, though he must know a greased palm often made impossible things possible.

Victor scratched his neck as he nodded.

"Yes. I must wed before the sixteenth of August, and I wasn't certain how long it would take me to find a bride. In the event there wasn't enough time to have the banns read, I had a special license prepared, just in case. Now I'd like to use it to join with Miss Brentwood in marriage."

"Then I regret to tell you that you've come in vain." Mr. Brentwood repeatedly rubbed his fingers across his thumb, definitely not as collected as he would have Victor believe. "I've promised her to Mr. Leadford, and my . . . *um* . . . honor requires I keep my word."

His honor or something else?

"With all due respect, Mr. Brentwood, I'm

offering Theadosia multiple titles, a life of comfort and privilege, and the means to assist her family. I am also prepared to bestow a five-thousand-pound dowry and a house in Bath upon Miss Jessica."

A noise echoed outside the door, and Victor angled his ear toward the panel.

Was someone listening at the keyhole?

After a moment, the reverend drew his gaze from the door. Not a doubt he'd heard the commotion as well.

"I appreciate your generosity, but Jessica, like Theadosia, will marry a man of the cloth, and therefore, has no need for a large dowry."

Moisture beaded Mr. Brentwood's upper lip, and he wouldn't meet Victor's eyes as he switched from fidgeting with his fingers to brushing his thumb against the pages of the open Bible he must've been reading when Victor interrupted.

Was this only about his daughters marrying clergymen?

Then why the uneasiness?

Victor rested his elbows on the arms of the chair

and hooked an ankle over his knee.

He would poke the lion and see what he stirred.

"I'll also pay for a complete upgrade and refurbishing of the parsonage, Church, and grounds."

Extreme perhaps, but since its inception, the duchy had supported the church. There'd been no major improvements in decades, and in truth, a renovation was past due.

That offer gave the reverend pause.

An enthusiastic sparkle entered his eyes as he swept a swift glance about the fusty office and then the Church, visible through tall, narrow windows. He drew in a deep breath and pressed his fingers to his temple, his expression contemplative.

Only a self-centered cull would deny his family and parishioners what Victor proposed.

Only a selfish cull bartered for a bride as if she were a piece of property sold to the highest bidder.

True, but this was for Thea's own good.

Releasing a resigned sigh, his shoulders slumping the merest bit, Reverend Brentwood shook his head once. A guarded look returned to his squarish features.

"Again, I must refuse your magnanimous offer, Your Grace."

Of its own accord, one of Victor's brows flew high on his forehead.

Was the man dicked in the nob?

It was one thing to be zealous about one's beliefs—that, Victor could respect and even admire—but it was another entirely to force a daughter to marry a man she clearly loathed. Especially when the match would not improve her position or benefit anyone except the reprobate marrying her.

"You would deny your daughters the opportunity to improve their stations?"

The words had no sooner left his mouth than Victor realized how arrogant they sounded and that he'd made a grave mistake.

"What I mean is—"

Mr. Brentwood slammed his hand down, rattling the ink pot, and shot straight upward. Bracing his hands upon the desk, he glowered down at Victor, his contempt palpable.

"I know precisely what you meant. That a mere

member of the clergy, a humble man, a poor man, is inferior to your blue-blooded peerage and heavy purse. You've wasted your time and mine, sir. Theadosia will marry Mr. Leadford as soon as the banns are read."

Victor laced his fingers and considered the cleric.

"She doesn't love him, and in fact, is afraid of him. Terrified, I'd say."

That truth had been as glaringly apparent as the god-awful blemish on Leadford's chin last night.

"And do *you* profess love for her, Your Grace?"

A sneer curled the reverend's upper lip as he regarded Victor with the revulsion he might a pimp siskin.

"Perhaps not love—*yet*—but I have immense regard for her and want to provide for her and protect her."

"And you think Leadford does not? *He,* at least, professes affection."

"Leadford might be a man of the cloth," Victor said, "but he is not the more honorable between us, as I believe you are already aware."

"Honor?" Casting his mocking gaze heavenward,

Mr. Brentwood choked on a scoff.

"God above, *he s*peaks of honor.

"Even in Colchester, Duke, your sinful *exploits* are known. You're a womanizer and a drunkard. Did you really think I didn't see the whisky bottle Theadosia tried to hide? You dared to blaspheme holy ground with the devil's drink, and persuaded her to aid you in your irreverence."

And yet, the good reverend had kept his silence these past days.

Why?

Because Victor was paying for the new organ and choir robes. That said much about the man of *God's* character and his priorities.

The nostrils of Brentwood's wide nose flared, revealing an abundance of unattractive hair. "I also know you kissed her. Treated my Theadosia like a common strumpet."

Another muffled bump echoed through the study door.

Whoever eavesdropped had ceased being covert.

"The Nabity sisters told me so the other day." The

reverend shook his head and slammed his fist atop his open Bible, crinkling the page. "I vow, I shan't have another daughter sullied by a handsome face."

Victor refused to discuss the kiss and have it reduced to a tawdry episode.

It had been a taste of pure heaven, and despite the impropriety, he didn't regret it. Theadosia had enjoyed it too, and he clamped his jaw to refrain from telling the rector to bugger himself for daring to use Thea's name and strumpet in the same sentence.

Victor neither frequented brothels nor dallied with harlots. The risk of disease was too great. Besides, now he had a killer disease in his bloodline to fret about.

"All the more reason Theadosia and I should wed at once to prevent any tainting of her reputation—as well as yours and the parish's." That latter might be a trifle overdone, but he wasn't leaving anything to chance.

Cutting his hand sharply through the air, Brentwood shook his head in disdain. "She's Miss Brentwood to you, and she's not one of your whores to be tossed aside when you grow bored with her. I don't doubt for a moment you'd resume your lascivious lifestyle within weeks of marrying her."

Damnation. That was exactly what Victor had planned to do, but that was before he'd decided to make Thea his wife.

"Your accusations and concerns are just. I've not lived a monk's life, but I give you my word upon my father's grave and the dukedom, that I would be faithful to her. I hold Theadosia in the highest esteem and would never deliberately cause her sorrow."

But do I love her?

How could he so soon?

For certain, he felt something compelling, and it wasn't just lust. He was quite familiar with *that* carnal urge. But was it love?

It mattered naught.

He'd do what he must to keep her safe from Leadford. And if, after they'd married, she wanted a divorce, he'd grant her one.

If she'd have him and agreed to, Victor would elope with her today. They could be across the border and wed within hours.

God, to see Leadford's face when they returned. Victor could savor that satisfaction for a great while.

"I cannot believe you, as a loving father, would force Thea to wed against her will." He wasn't ready to toss in his cards just yet. If Brentwood insisted on this ridiculousness, he'd do so knowing others were well aware of what he was making Thea to do.

"It's no concern of yours." Face a mottled red, Mr. Brentwood ran a finger between his cravat and neck, then wiped his brow and upper lip with his handkerchief. Did he always sweat buckets or only when under fire?

"Now I shall bid you good day," Brentwood said, scarcely this side of civil. "I have a sermon to finish preparing."

Victor rose and after pulling his jacket into place, cocked his head.

The reverend fidgeted with his Bible, looking everywhere but at him.

"Doesn't your honor and paternal affection demand you consider your daughter's happiness? Would you subject her to a lifetime of misery? Surely you know, or at least suspect, what type of wretch Leadford is. He'll abuse her for certain. Can you live with that knowledge?"

Jaw slack, Brentwood paled to a ghastly shade before summoning his bluster once more.

"Do not presume to impugn my integrity. I know what is best for my daughter. You are no longer welcome in this house, and I forbid you to see or speak to Theadosia. I cannot in good conscience ban you from attending church services, lest your immortal soul suffer, but you shall not approach her."

Something suspicious was going on here. The reverend was far too overwrought. Far too defensive and irrational. Like a man concealing a dark secret. Something that might ruin him and his way of life if it became known.

James might be just the person to prod around a bit in that area. Horse's hooves had echoed in the drive a few moments ago. Hopefully it was James returning home, and before departing, Victor intended to have a word.

"I've known you to be a reasonable man my entire

life, Reverend. Always fair and just, if a trifle hard and unyielding at times. This community and your parish respect you, as much for your dedication to them and your position as for your commitment to your family. The Reverend Brentwood I know would never force his daughter into a loveless marriage, much less with a man who gropes her whenever you aren't looking."

Mr. Brentwood's head jerked up, and his gaze clashed with Victor's. Within the clergyman's gaze, anguish warred with indecision and . . . *fear?*

Did Leadford have something on him?

He must.

What the hell would cause Mr. Brentwood to sacrifice a daughter to a man of Leadford's character?

Victor extended a hand, palm upward. "Mr. Brentwood, I can help you, but only if you tell me what is going on."

Self-righteous outrage snuffed out the other conflicting emotions from the reverend's countenance.

Pride would be the cleric's downfall. He'd do anything to save face. Even subject Thea to a debaucher.

"Once more you cross the mark, Your Grace." His hand unsteady, Mr. Brentwood pointed to the door. "Please leave before I forget I'm a man of God and lose my temper entirely. My daughter is none of your concern."

We'll see about that.

Victor strode to the exit. His earlier anxiety had dissipated, and he had one focus now.

Protect Theadosia at all costs.

Was whoever who'd been listening still outside?

Making a pretense of grasping the handle and wiggling it, he gave whoever it was time to flee. If he had to guess, he'd vow Miss Jessica couldn't contain her curiosity. Hopefully, she'd repeat everything to Thea.

This wasn't over.

No, indeed.

Never before had Victor's ability to keenly read people been as important. It was what gave him such an advantage at cards and other gaming, and was one of the reasons he'd been able to amass his fortune.

In the past fifteen minutes he'd learned something

interesting.

He opened the door, and after checking to be sure the corridor was empty, faced Mr. Brentwood.

"Leadford's blackmailing you, isn't he?"

8

Why had Victor sought an audience with Papa?

Fighting back stinging tears for the umpteenth time since last night, Theadosia marched through the Fielding's apple and pear orchard, her basket rhythmically thumping against her hip as she trudged along. She refused to succumb to the moisture prickling behind her eyelids. She wasn't a blasted watering pot.

When Jessica had rushed into the garden and told her Victor had called, asking to speak to their father, Theadosia's heart had dared accelerate in hope. For what, she wasn't certain, but Victor had seen her desperation last night.

He'd given the slightest nod when she'd mouthed, "Help me."

It was much too brazen of her. She'd no right to ask it of him, but from the moment he'd re-entered her life, she'd trusted him more than any other person. Although they'd only spent a few days together, she believed he would aid her.

Then, first thing this morning, he appeared at the parsonage door. Surely that must mean he'd found a way out of her horrible dilemma.

She could not—would not—marry Mr. Leadford.

How could Papa expect such a thing?

If she refused, would he disown her as he had Althea?

Her situation wasn't the same at all. Her sister had eloped with a man she adored, but Theadosia was being forced to marry a sod she loathed. Nonetheless, her father expected blind obedience from his daughters, especially after Althea's betrayal.

He might very well chastise Mama for allowing Theadosia to leave the house on this errand. When she'd swooned last night—a first for her—he'd been livid that she'd humiliated him thusly. Oh, he hadn't permitted the duke and duchess to see his ire, but the instant they'd settled into the carriage, he'd threatened to lock her in her room until the wedding.

Mama, angrier than Theadosia had ever seen her, had called him an unreasonable tyrant and presented him the back of her head. This morning, she still wasn't speaking to him.

That was also a first.

Mama must've known Theadosia needed to escape the house, especially after she'd seen Victor sitting in Papa's study. Her mother had defied Papa and sent Theadosia to deliver a cold meal to the Fieldings. Plump, cheerful, and obviously adored by her equally jolly and rotund husband, Mrs. Fielding had delivered her fifth child yesterday.

Theadosia loved children, especially babies, but she'd rather become a dried up, shriveled prune-of-a-spinster than allow Mr. Leadford to bed her.

A forceful shudder rippled down her spine at the disgusting notion, and she hunched deeper into her spencer.

She'd brought a shawl today as well, but in her haste to leave the parish, had forgotten her bonnet. This summer was proving to be one of the coolest she could ever remember. However, revulsion rather than the disagreeable weather caused the chill juddering her spine.

Drawing in a deep breath, she ordered her careening thoughts to order. Responding like a ninny wasn't going to help the situation.

A plan. That was what she needed. A logical plan.

And she needed one speedily.

On the ride home last evening, her father had declared he intended to read the banns for the first time this Sunday. If Victor hadn't persuaded him otherwise during his visit, that was.

How she'd wanted to slap Mr. Leadford's smug face as he leaned against the squabs, all self-satisfied arrogance. She'd bet her boot buttons he'd orchestrated this, but how, in such a short time?

Another wave of frustration engulfed her.

How could Papa be so callous? So hard-hearted?

How could he completely disregard her feelings

and wishes? What possible reason could there be for rushing the nuptials? She scarce knew Mr. Leadford.

She might argue the same about Victor, but that was much different. She enjoyed his company and anticipated seeing him. When she wasn't with Victor, her thoughts continually drifted toward him. Upon first awakening, he infiltrated her mind, and as she drifted off to sleep, he hovered on the perimeters of her consciousness.

Now she understood why Althea had fled with Antione Nasan, a French artist who'd been sketching likenesses with a traveling troupe. He'd approached Papa and asked for her hand in marriage. Papa had all but thrown him out of the house, and he *had* locked Althea in her room. Two nights later, she'd picked the lock and fled with her lover.

Jessica and Theadosia had kept watch to make sure Papa didn't catch her. He had no idea they'd conspired together. Theadosia suspected Mama knew the truth, but she'd never hinted at any such thing.

Theadosia inhaled deeply again, savoring the earthy aroma beneath the gnarled trees where a few wax cap mushrooms had sprung up. Mere weeks ago, these same trees had dripped with fragrant pinkish-white blossoms, promising an abundance of fruit this autumn. Unless Papa changed his mind about her marrying Mr. Leadford, she wouldn't be here for the harvest.

If she must, she'd run away.

To Althea in France.

Just this morning, in a hushed whisper, her mother had confessed she'd secretly been writing to Althea and receiving letters in return. Althea had two little boys, and her husband had become a successful portrait painter. For months, she'd been begging Mama to visit and bring Jessica and Theadosia.

Her mother hadn't dared.

Risking Papa's fury, James had helped Mama and Althea correspond.

He'd help Theadosia escape too. She didn't doubt it.

But to never see her mother or Jessica again? That risk was very real. A probability, unless Papa died.

Pain stabbed Theadosia to her core, and she

slapped a hand to her middle, gasping at the agony of that awful truth.

There must be another way.

How could Althea bear it?

Because she had a man who loved her and whom she loved in return.

Tears threatened again, but Theadosia swiped them away.

As she climbed the gentle slope toward the lane leading to the Fielding's house, she caught a movement from the corner of her eye.

Alarm skittered across her shoulders, and she whirled to face her stalker.

"Why are you following me, Mr. Leadford?"

He emerged from behind one of the gnarled old apple trees and offered a repentant smile.

"I was looking for an opportunity to speak with you but feared I'd startle you." He thrust a handful of blossoms toward her. "Here, I picked you flowers."

Likely filched from the Church's gardens.

Sliding the basket onto her other arm, she made a pretense of adjusting the cloth covering the food and grasped the bottle of lemonade. She'd not hesitate to crack him over the nog with it if he attempted to accost her.

"So, you skulk about like a thief? Couldn't you have waited until I returned home?"

Skewing a brow, she leveled him a dubious look, but made no effort to take the fast-wilting blooms.

She didn't like being alone with him one jot, and the Fielding's house was still a quarter of a mile away. He'd already proved he was no gentleman.

If only she had told Mama about his harassment. She would've sent Jessica too. Except Theadosia had really wanted to be alone to sort out her thoughts.

Angling away, she dismissed him. "I must go. The Fieldings expected me some time ago, and my mother awaits my return. We've preserves to make."

Not exactly the truth, but he needn't know that.

"Permit me to accompany you." He hurried to reach her side, his gaze straying to her breasts.

He tried to lay the flowers in the basket, frowning when she drew it away.

"I don't like my betrothed walking about

unescorted."

"As to that, we are not officially betrothed, and I intend to do everything in my power to see that we never are." She tightened her grip on the bottle. Though not nearly as large as the duke, Mr. Leadford wasn't a simpering fop either. He could easily overpower her. "I'd prefer to walk alone, if you don't mind" *And even if you do.* "I've done so dozens of times without fear of harm."

"But I do mind." He grasped her elbow, none too gently, and yanked her to his chest. Triumph glittered in his frosty blue eyes.

His reptilian smile sent a ripple of stark fear through her.

"You *will* marry me, Theadosia. I have the means to force you to."

"I don't think so."

They whirled to see a hatless and gloveless Duke of Sutcliffe sauntering up the hill.

Despite his leisurely approach, his chest rose and fell quickly as if he'd been hurrying. Everything about him shouted masculine animal grace, but primal danger exuded from him too. His gaze took in the hand gripping Theadosia's arm, and the murderous look he leveled Mr. Leadford caused another hair-raising shiver to scuttle across her shoulders.

He wasn't a man to cross, and she was glad his ire was directed at Mr. Leadford.

"Release her, Leadford."

In three more long-legged strides Victor was upon them.

Mr. Leadford drew himself up, retaining his harsh grip upon her arm.

He shook the flowers at Victor. "I'm her betrothed, and it's my right—"

"I told you to release her."

Victor stepped nearer, and Mr. Leadford's bravado slipped a jot. He didn't back away or relinquish his hold, but his Adam's apple bobbed up and down like a frightened mouse caught on a shelf, and his shifty gaze skittered about as if determining the quickest escape route.

In a deadly calm but unyielding voice, Victor said, "You are not formally betrothed, and as she objects to your touch, you are accosting her." He glanced at Theadosia for confirmation, and she gave a vehement nod. "Perhaps the magistrate should be informed. Doubtful you'd retain your position afterward."

That did it.

Mr. Leadford retreated a step but wasn't ready to quit the field just yet, it seemed.

"I do not appreciate your interference, Sutcliffe. We are betrothed. Her father verbally contracted with me, and the rest is just formalities." Again, he waggled the poor abused blossoms.

Theadosia released her vice-like grip on the bottle while edging closer to Victor.

He promptly tucked her hand into the crook of his elbow and held it to his side. Something a long-time married couple might do.

At once, her fear dissipated, to be replaced by the familiar sensation of coming home she experienced each time he touched her.

"It's Your Grace to you, and *I* don't appreciate *you* waylaying Miss Brentwood with your unwanted attention."

His glare murderous, Leadford jerked his chin up, an unfortunate decision, since it drew attention to the impossibly large boil there.

"That's because you want her for yourself." Again, Theadosia longed to slap the smug half-smile from his face. "I heard you offer for her, but Brentwood turned you down flat."

Something hot and gratifying blazed behind her breastbone. Theadosia searched Victor's striking features, afraid to believe what she'd just heard.

"Listening at the keyhole, were you?" He flicked Leadford a contemptuous glance. "Why am I not surprised?"

"You truly asked for my hand?" That dream had finally become a reality, if for all the wrong reasons, and her father had squelched it without regard to her desires.

Victor spared her a brief glance and a fond smile. "Yes, I did."

That was how he'd intended to help her?

Leadford's gloating laugh disturbed the orchard's tranquility.

"You couldn't even buy her hand for all of your illustrious titles and riches. You were so pathetic, all but begging, offering to dower her sister and refurbish the parsonage and Church. And Brentwood still said no."

Mr. Leadford laughed again, this one more maniacal than humorous.

He's mad. Dear God, Papa has promised me to a madman.

Theadosia shrank into Victor's side, and he wrapped his arm about her waist.

At Victor's boldness, Leadford balled his fists, crushing the flower's stems. His face glowing crimson, his chest rising and falling with his heavy breathing.

"He also forbade you to see her, and you can be sure I'll tell him you ignored him."

Victor didn't flinch under Mr. Leadford's verbal assault. In fact, his cool control was a stark contrast to the curate's flushed-faced agitation.

"I'm counting on it. And you can tell him I'll continue to do so until *she* tells me to stop."

"Which I never will." That truth might as well be

known.

The delighted smile Victor bestowed upon her did all sorts of peculiar things to her insides.

"You heard her. Do be a good fellow and be gone." Victor jerked his head in the direction he'd just come. "My patience wears thin."

A robin red breast swooped from an apple tree and began poking about the soil a few feet away.

Leadford tossed the flowers to the ground, and the panicked bird took to the air with an outraged chirrup.

"She is mine, Sutcliffe, do you hear me? Theadosia is mine. In a matter of weeks, she will be in *my* bed, pleasuring *me*. Won't that gnaw at you? Me, the lowly clergyman, rogering her day and night, anywhere and any time I desire. Getting her with child, over and over."

"Never," Theadosia and Victor said simultaneously.

Victor splayed his fingers across her ribs, the movement thrilling and soothing at the same time. "I shall make Thea my wife, Leadford. You'd best prepare yourself for that eventuality."

She nodded her head, finally allowing her revulsion for Leadford to show. "I would never marry you. Never."

A self-satisfied smile replaced Leadford's fury. All smug superiority, he bent one knee and rested a hand on his hip.

"Not even to keep your precious Papa from prison?"

Theadosia stiffened, her heart diving to her belly. She cut Victor a swift worried glance before wetting her lower lip. She didn't want to ask, dreading the answer, but she must know.

"Just what are you implying?"

"It's quite simple, my dear. If you don't marry me, I'll reveal what I know, and your father will go to prison for a very, *very* long time." He clutched his throat theatrically. "Why, he might even . . . *hang*."

Theadosia jerked as if skewered.

"I don't believe you. Papa would never do anything immoral or illegal."

Except . . . these past few days he *had* been out of sorts. Like a man carrying a tremendous burden. Oh

God, was there truth to Leadford's despicable accusation?

"All men are capable of treachery if circumstances decree it. Could you live with yourself, Theadosia? Knowing you could have prevented your father's fate? Knowing your mother and sister will be cast out of their home, disgraced and impoverished? And to think, you might've alleviated their hardships by being unselfish and wedding me."

What he said couldn't be true.

Her father valued honesty and integrity above all else.

Leadford brushed his hands down the front of his simple black coat, ridding the fabric of a couple of stray petals. "If I weren't a moral man, I wouldn't bother marrying you. Your father would've still agreed to give you to me, though. You should know that."

"No," she breathed.

Even as she denied his claim, she knew he probably spoke the truth.

"One more word, Leadford, and I'll lay you out flat."

Voice gravelly with barely suppressed fury, Victor lunged forward a pace.

"*Tsk*, Your Grace. Such a violent temper. I'll pray for that vice along with *all* of your others. Now I'll leave you to say your farewells. You won't be seeing each other again. I'll see to that. I'm off to inform the reverend of your clandestine meeting. I shouldn't be the least surprised if he locks you in your room and sends me to acquire a special license straightaway, *my dear*."

"You are vile through and through." On the cusp of completely losing her composure, Theadosia averted her face.

"Just think, *sweetheart*, we might be wed within a day." Leering, he leaned forward into her line of vision. "Oh, by the by, I expect a virgin in my bed, else I'll have to tell the authorities what I know about the Honorable Oscar Brentwood. Such a shame if we're wed and dear Papa finds himself imprisoned anyway."

After another gloating grin, he gave a jaunty wave and made his way down the hillside.

Unmoving, unable to rip her focus away, she

watched, unblinking until he disappeared from sight. She inhaled a wobbly breath and pressed her fingertips to her forehead.

"That's why my father insists I marry him," she managed through her tear-clogged throat. "Papa has committed some sort of crime."

9

Shutting her eyes, Theadosia battled despair.

How could she send her father to prison? Or worse?

"I don't know what to do, Victor. I cannot allow Papa to be imprisoned or risk him hanging. Nor can I see Mama and Jessica turned out into the street, destitute, though I'm confident James would help. But life with that wretched excuse of humanity would be utterly unbearable. It makes me positively ill to think of . . ."

Her flesh shrank in repulsion when Leadford gazed at her. How could she ever tolerate his touch?

A tear leaked from her eye, and Victor brushed it

away with his thumb. He gathered her into his arms and kissed the hair near her temple.

"Don't under-estimate my power and connections, darling. Leadford is blackmailing your father. I deduced that much this morning. We have to find out what for, and toward that end, I've enlisted your brother's help. Leadford won't stop after forcing you to marry him. He'll continue with the extortion. Your father must be made to see the only way out of this cesspool is for him to come clean and confess whatever it is that he's done."

Eyes still closed, she relished the comfort of his embrace.

"Why is he so determined to have me? We've only known each other a short while, but I saw something in his eyes that first day. He's obsessed, and it's terrifying. I don't know what he's capable of." She shuddered and burrowed deeper into Victor's chest.

She'd only been reacquainted with him for the same amount of time, and yet she was more comfortable with him than any other person, including Jessica.

"I suspect, my sweet, he's after the rectorship, the Church, all of it. All Saint's is a wealthy parish." Victor kissed her temple again whilst running his hand up and down her ribs. "I also believe he's unhinged. I sent a letter to a friend of mine, the Duke of Westfall, a few days ago. You'll meet him at the ball."

"*If* I go—" She started to protest.

He shushed her with a fingertip to her lips. "You *will* attend."

His confidence did him credit, but he didn't know her father as she did.

"As I was saying," Victor said, "Westfall enjoys dabbling in amateur investigative work, and I've asked him to poke around and see what he can uncover about Leadford. Something stinks to high heaven regarding that churl."

"Victor, I didn't expect you to ask for my hand when I asked you for help."

Theadosia spoke into his delicious, manly smelling, oh-so-firm chest. She could stand like this for hours. For a lifetime.

"Believe me, I wanted to, and I wouldn't have

done so if I hadn't. I've been entertaining the idea since I first kissed you." He tilted her chin upward, his penetrating gaze probing hers. His held a tantalizing promise. "Which I intend to do again. Now."

"Oh, yes. Please."

She raised her mouth to his, sighing when his lips met hers. This kiss was different than the first, more reverent, but simmering with restrained passion nonetheless.

With a guttural groan, Victor crushed her to his chest and plundered her mouth. His tongue swept hers, and she instinctively met each thrust.

Only the clanking of the basket's contents drew her reluctant attention away from his blistering kisses. Giving a shaky laugh, she jostled the container. "I almost dropped this, and poor Mrs. Fielding needs all the respite she can get with five little ones now."

Victor framed her face between his hands, his expression so earnest Theadosia's heart cramped.

"Thea, elope with me to Gretna Green. Today. I can have a carriage readied within the hour."

"Your chivalry is touching and appreciated,

Victor, but what kind of a woman would I be if I allowed you to make such a sacrifice for me? You were to pick your bride at the ball, remember? I'm hardly duchess material."

"Trust me, darling, it's no sacrifice. I adore you and want to marry you. I intended to ask you at the ball. I've not been able to get you out of my thoughts since we met in the cemetery. When I try to sleep, you invade my dreams. When I'm looking through account ledgers, I lose track of where I am, because I keep remembering our kiss. If we eloped, you'd be safe from Leadford for now and always."

Feeling like she might fragment, she forced her mouth into a smile and laid her palm against his cheek. Even through her glove she felt the bristly, dark stubble shadowing his lean jaw. Was he a man who had to shave more than once a day?

As he had in the churchyard, he gripped her hand and bent his shiny midnight head to kiss the inside of her wrist.

"I cannot, Victor. Not until I know what Leadford is using to blackmail Papa. I shan't be the cause of my father's imprisonment." She couldn't even contemplate him hanging. "Nor can I face being shunned by my family. You don't know Papa. He's uncompromising. We're not even allowed to say Althea's name. If you and I wed and he doesn't go to prison, I mightn't ever see my mother or sister again."

How could she choose between the man she loved and her mother and sister?

Could James be persuaded to arrange clandestine meetings?

Would Mama flout Papa in that matter too?

Victor's feature's tightened.

"You are not the cause of your father's dilemma. The reverend's done something, likely criminal, and Leadford knows what it is." Condemnation tightened his features, and his voice took on the harsh note she'd come to recognize as a sign of controlled ire. "Your father has only himself to blame, and it's cruel to keep you from seeing Althea. Where's the forgiveness he preaches from his pulpit?"

"Everything you say is true, but he's still my father, Victor, and I love him despite his faults. Surely you can understand that after your father—."

"I know, and I do understand." He kissed her forehead and breathed out a deep sigh. "Fine. We don't elope, but will you marry me, Thea? And trust me to help your father?"

"I want to say yes, Victor. I truly do." She dropped her gaze as a blush heated her cheeks. "I've dreamed of becoming your wife for a very long time."

There, she'd said it.

Given him a hint as to her feelings. A union between them might be a marriage of convenience for him, but for her it would be a love match.

"You have? Truly?"

The hot, hungry gleam in his steel grey eyes nearly unhinged her knees. He captured her mouth in another sizzling kiss, and several blissful moments passed before he reluctantly lifted his lips.

"I cannot tell you how happy it makes me to know you've thought about becoming my wife. I didn't want a cold, affectionless union, but feared I'd have to settle for one. I know we can be very happy together."

For the first time, she allowed the love she'd kept hidden to show in the adoring gaze she lifted to him. He hadn't said he loved her, but his joy at her declaration surely meant he also had feelings for her, didn't it?

"Then yes, I shall marry you."

He cupped the back of her head with his strong hand, tenderness softening his features. "We must wed by August sixteenth or all of my unentailed properties and monies are awarded to my cousin. My mother would have to vacate Ridgewood Court, and I shan't let that happen."

Victor had to marry to keep from being disinherited?

Her earlier euphoria melted away.

There was nothing chivalrous or gallant about that.

She'd known from the beginning that he must wed swiftly. He was a far better choice than Mr. Leadford, and she'd be an idealistic ninnyhammer to reject his offer—even if she was simply a means to an end for him.

"August sixteenth? But . . . that's only a few

weeks away."

"It is, and I *shall* be married by then."

A moment ago, Theadosia's heart had been so full she almost wept, and now she wanted to sob from heartbreak. She leaned away from his forceful embrace, dreading his answer, but she must have the truth.

"Are you saying if this business with my father isn't settled in a month, and I cannot marry you yet, you'll wed another?"

His expression grim, Victor nodded.

"I don't wish that, but I am honor-bound to protect my mother even as you must protect your father." Even to his own ears, it sounded weak and unconvincing.

She edged away, her heart fracturing more with each retreating step.

"You're marrying to retain wealth and property and to keep your mother in her opulent mansion. I'm being forced to wed a reprobate to keep my father out of prison and to prevent my mother and sister from becoming homeless."

She shook her head, a tear trailing down her cheek.

"They are not the same things at all, Victor. I was a naive fool to think I was anything other than a convenient means to an end for you."

Her heart heavier than it had been when she left the parsonage that morning, Theadosia sighed as she pushed open the kitchen door. The scent of fresh-baked bread, and what smelled like a beef roast filled the warm room. She hadn't eaten today, and normally the scrumptious smells would have sent her in search of a biscuit or two.

Not after her heartbreaking departure from Victor.

He hadn't denied her accusation. He'd just stood there, his handsome face hard and uncompromising, as she walked away, each step rendering another crack in her heart.

Though he professed to want to marry her, he'd marry another to keep his money and property and to protect his mother.

The duchess didn't face imprisonment or hanging. She might have to live in a different mansion. So blasted what? She'd still live a pampered, privileged life.

Reason whispered the hard, inescapable truth.

Victor couldn't be expected to wait and sacrifice his inheritance or his mother's home on the chance Theadosia escaped the fate her father had orchestrated for her.

He'd vowed he'd do everything within his power to uncover the truth.

But how long would that take?

Weeks?

Months?

She didn't have the latter.

To lose Victor before he was even hers ripped her heart ragged about the edges.

After setting the basket atop the worktable, she pushed the loose curls off her forehead and headed toward the bedchamber she shared with Jessica.

She wanted to think, and she urgently needed to

speak with James. He must be told what had happened.

Had Mr. Leadford already tattled to her father as he'd threatened?

Would Papa truly lock her in her room?

Yes. He had Althea.

Theadosia's situation was impossible. No matter what she decided, she'd hurt someone she loved. She'd have to choose the lesser of two evils, and either would leave scars and a broken heart.

Protect my mother even as you must protect your father.

Victor's words played through her mind once more, all but ripping her aching heart from her chest.

As she neared the staircase, Mama's angry voice carried down the corridor.

"You've gone too far this time, Oscar. I didn't agree when you banished Althea, and I surely shan't stand by and watch you force Theadosia into a marriage with a despicable man I cannot abide."

Theadosia crept down the corridor on tip-toes, mindful to avoid the squeaky floorboards. As she reached the drawing room, Jessica edged from the adjacent doorway, a finger to her lips.

She silently urged Theadosia inside the study.

"They've been arguing almost since you left," Jessica whispered in her ear.

"Has Mr. Leadford returned?"

Jessica shook her head, the blond curls framing her face bouncing.

"No, but that's the reason I'm hiding in here. If he comes back, I want to make sure he doesn't eavesdrop." Color swept up her cheeks. "I know I am guilty of the doing same, but I'm doing so because I want to help. He'd only use whatever he hears for his own gain."

No small truth there.

Tears filled Jessica's eyes. "Lord, I cannot abide the man, and I cannot bear the idea that you might have to wed him. He's a disgusting pig."

Wrapping an arm around her sister's waist, Theadosia gave her a hug. "I'm going into the drawing room. Mama and Papa are discussing my future. Yours too. I cannot stand idly by and not voice my opinion. Besides, I saw Leadford a bit ago, and he threatened me and Papa."

Jessica's pretty eyes widened, and her jaw sagged. "I knew he was evil."

"You have no idea just how much so." Theadosia shuddered in remembrance.

Best not to mention Victor had also been there or his proposal. Theadosia knew what her sweet sister would say about that.

A horrible thought struck her, stealing her breath.

If she married Victor, might Leadford turn his vulgar attention to Jessica?

Another reason she could not marry Victor straightaway.

"I'm taking our daughters, and we're going to live with James until you come to your senses." Mama's voice broke. "Wasn't losing one daughter enough, Oscar? I cannot lose another."

Didn't Mama know James let lodgings at the Albany? He didn't have room for them, and Theadosia didn't think women were permitted to reside there either.

"I'm coming with you," Jessica said, with a

determined tilt of her small chin.

Theadosia grasped her hand, and mouth flattened into a firm line, entered the room.

"You cannot leave with Theadosia, Marianne. It's impossible."

Father sank into a chair, and raising a shaking hand to his ashen face, knuckled away a tear.

"Why not, Papa? Why have you promised me to Mr. Leadford when you know I detest him?"

Theadosia, holding Jessica's hand, hovered at the entrance.

Startled, he glanced up for an instant, then dropped his gaze to his lap and said nothing.

When had he become a coward?

Face taut, Mama also looked toward the doorway. She motioned to the faded settee before the window. "You might as well come in since this involves you both."

Though Theadosia felt a degree of compassion for her father, he'd put her in a horrible predicament. He must own his wrongdoing and acknowledge his selfishness.

After taking a seat, she met his doleful gaze straight on. "Mr. Leadford says if I don't marry him, you will go to prison. You might even hang."

"God above, Oscar, what have you done?" Mama, asked, her voice breaking again. Pale as her lace fichu, she stiffly lowered herself to a chair. Pressing an unsteady palm to her chest, she swallowed.

Jessica squeezed Theadosia's fingers as Papa stared out the window, his face creased and haggard.

"I thought that if I provided Theadosia and Jessica with some of the luxuries young women like, they mightn't be tempted to sin as Althea was." He slid them a repentant look.

Hence the new gowns and fripperies.

"I understand it's hard being a rector's wife and children," he murmured, his voice so low, Theadosia had to strain to hear him. "I also know that I give our food and other belongings, even money, to the poor to such an extent that we must economize. We must go without and live a simple, frugal life. But I also realize women want pretty things, and the girls were getting of an age, I feared they'd look for the wrong type of young man, as Althea did."

Her father's generosity had been out of character, but Theadosia hadn't questioned where he'd acquired the funds for their new garments, bonnets, and shoes these past few months. She'd assumed he'd received an increase in wages.

"We mightn't wear the first stare of fashion or eat delicacies, but we've always had enough. So what exactly are you saying, Oscar?"

Mama wasn't letting him transfer the blame to them.

Head lowered, he covered his eyes with his fingertips.

"I've been borrowing from the tithes and organ fund, and also keeping monies I said were sent to the Diocese," he admitted, still not meeting their gazes. "It's been six months since Benedict left, and I didn't think Leadford would notice the small discrepancies in the account ledgers. I swear I meant to pay back every penny."

So livid, her red hair almost crackled with her ire, Mama narrowed her eyes. "You've been gambling again too, haven't you? Just like before we moved here."

Papa's chin sank to his chest, and his shoulders slumped. "Yes."

Mama's lips trembled, and she shook her head. "You swore to me, Oscar. On the Bible. You vowed you'd *never* touch dice again."

Theadosia exchanged a dumbfounded glance with Jessica. Papa a gambler?

"How much, Oscar?" Mama demanded. "How much have you stolen?"

"Leadford says it's almost five hundred pounds."

Five hundred? It might as well be five thousand.

Jessica gasped, and Mama collapsed against her chair.

"I don't remember taking that much." Papa had never been very good at bookkeeping or figures, something he readily admitted to. "I have repaid a little from my wages."

James strode into the drawing room, his expression fierce.

"Did I hear correctly? You've been embezzling

Church funds and gambling? To the tune of five hundred pounds?" He made a disgusted noise in the back of his throat and whirled away from Papa. Plowing a hand through his hair, he spun back to face him again.

"My God, Father. Do you have any idea how harsh the courts are on men of the cloth?" James threw his hands in the air. "Men who preach righteousness and honesty and then betray the Church's and their parish's trust?"

Theadosia rubbed her temple. This was much more awful than she'd imagined.

"You realize Leadford won't stop at marrying me, don't you? You'll be under his thumb, groveling about whenever he decides he wants something more. You've ruined us, Papa. How will we ever be free of him?"

Her father raised his eyes, his harrowed expression fraught with shame. He glanced first at Mama's stricken face, then at Jessica, and lastly at Theadosia.

"Forgive me, my dears." Moisture shimmered in his eyes. "It's even worse than that, I'm afraid."

"How could it possibly be worse?" Disbelief strangling his voice, James plopped onto the settee's arm.

"Leadford claims since the women used the stolen monies to buy gowns and fallalls, they are accessories to the crime." Entreaty in his gaze, Papa shrank into his chair. "If we don't do exactly as he demands, he vows to send your mother and sisters to prison too."

10

Two mornings later, after a pair of sleepless nights reliving Thea's last heart-wrenching words, Victor once again rapped on the doorframe outside the solarium's open door.

"Mother, a word if you've a moment."

She set aside her correspondence and, removing her spectacles, smiled warmly.

"Dearest, forgive me for saying so, but you look exhausted. Didn't you sleep well again last night?" She picked up the bell atop her petite writing desk. "Shall I ring Grover for coffee?"

"No, I've already had three cups, thick and black enough to tar a roof." He bent and kissed her upturned cheek. "I spent the night pacing my bedchamber, and I've come to a most difficult decision."

"Have a seat and tell me what has you so disgruntled. Has it to do with Theadosia?"

He gave her a sharp look.

How did she know?

"Don't look so taken aback, darling." She gave him one of her motherly smiles; the one that said she knew something he didn't think she did. "I saw how you gazed at her the other night. But there were also other hints as to your feelings."

"What hints? I've been most inconspicuous." Had even lied to himself about his motives and actions.

She held up her hand, fingers extended and ticked them off one by one.

"You impulsively invited the Brentwoods to dinner—you are never impulsive, dear." Thumb. "You asked that I be sure to invite them to the ball." Forefinger. "You asked me to make certain they would attend too. You also suggested I ask Theadosia to help me with the planning. You disappeared almost every day at the same time and were seen with her near

Bower Pool."

Middle finger, ring finger, and little finger, one right after the other.

She elevated a fine eyebrow. "The Walter boys' mother is sister to our larder maid."

Ah, the rascals had tattled to their mother.

His mother touched her other thumb with her pointer finger. "And from God knows where, you procured a case of oranges for marmalade."

She wiggled the beringed digits in front of his face. "You are clearly besotted, and I couldn't be happier for you. Especially since Theadosia obviously returns your affection."

He shook his head and chuckled. Did nothing escape his mother?

"I love her. I think I loved her before I left three years ago but didn't recognize that's what I felt."

"So why the glum face? You have your bride." She gave him a brilliant smile. "Should we make an announcement at the ball?"

"It's not that simple." He took a seat beside her, and as succinctly as possible, explained all.

"I knew there was something unsavory about that troll of a man." Lips pursed, she wrinkled her nose. "And to think he sat at my table. I shall instruct Grover to throw out the serviette he used."

How the butler was to tell the difference between that particular serviette and the other twenty or thirty, Victor couldn't imagine.

"I shall find a way to deal with Leadford," he said, "but I'm concerned about what this means for you."

She took his hand between hers.

"Victor, listen to me. I can make my home anywhere, as long as my children and grandchildren visit me often. Ridgewood is only a building. Yes, there are lots of wonderful memories here, but you love Theadosia. You must do everything to make her your duchess. If that means your birthday comes and goes and you are not wed, then so what? Jeffery will gain a fortune and several holdings. He'll be ecstatic. I never held with that addendum to the will anyway."

Was there ever a more wonderful mother?

"There will likely be a scandal, Mother. Scads of gossip and tattle-mongering when everything comes out. Rest assured, there will be those who say I've married beneath myself."

"Oh, pish posh. That always makes the romance more exciting. Why, I called off my betrothal to a Russian prince to marry your father. Cousin Cora was only too happy to take my place."

"Do tell. A Russian prince? I might've been a prince rather than a mere duke?"

"Constantine never stood a chance. He didn't hold a candle to your father's wicked good looks." She leaned forward and kissed Victor's cheek. "Now go be a hero. Women adore men coming to their rescue, but do let her think she helped too." She winked. "Now go, do whatever you must to save our dear Thea."

Two hours later, Victor handed Acheron's reins to a groom at the Blue Rose Inn at Essex Crossings. James had sent a missive 'round that morning saying he urgently needed to speak with his old friend.

Victor nodded to the patrons as he made his way to a table in the far corner.

James, his expression as morose as Victor had ever seen, stared into a tankard.

"I presume you don't have good news?"

James spared him a caustic glance before taking a long pull of ale. "No."

"What's happened?"

By the time James had finished speaking, Victor was hard put not to jump up and go in search of Leadford and rearrange his face. Instead, he quaffed back the rest of his ale.

"Is there any merit to what Leadford claims? Can the women be tried and convicted as accomplices?"

James slowly shook his head, his expression thoughtful.

"They can be tried, but Father has written a statement that he alone was responsible. As far as I know, Mama and the girls didn't have access to the books, though that might be hard to prove. The scandal would be horrendous, but I don't think they'd be convicted. Father would, however."

Victor hooked his arm over the back of his chair.

"What if I repay the funds and your father resigns effective immediately? I would even be willing to restore and refurbish the parsonage and Church. Do you think the Church would consider clemency then?"

That fell just short of bribery in Victor's estimation, but experience had taught him incentives went a long way. Even with those who claimed a Godly calling.

Folding his arms, James tilted his chair back. "Not as long as Leadford is around to stir things up." He sighed and scrubbed a hand across his eyes. "I'm not saying my father shouldn't take responsibility for what he's done, nor should he escape punishment. But we both know if he was a peer, he'd never see the inside of a cell."

Signaling the barkeep for another tankard, he looked toward Victor to see if he desired another as well.

Victor angled his head in affirmation.

"What if he was related to a peer? And if he agreed to do some sort of penance?"

"Maybe." Shrugging, James accepted the foamy tankard. The mug at his mouth, he paused and a teasing grin tipped his lips

"Wait. Related to a peer? You and Thea?"

183

"I already proposed. She said yes if this business with Leadford is settled. Your father, on the other hand, very vehemently said no." Victor stretched his legs out before him, one hand resting on the table. "I think he might be persuaded to change his mind if he weren't being coerced by Leadford."

James's smile widened, and he slapped his knee.

"I knew it. Thea couldn't keep her eyes off you, and you weren't any better. I must say, I couldn't have chosen anyone finer for her."

"Then you approve?" It was nice to have one Brentwood in his corner.

James still wore a silly smile. "Heartily."

"May I look at the accounts?" Victor asked.

"Of course. I did last evening. Honestly, they're such a scribbled mess, I cannot make heads or tails of them." James tossed a coin onto the table and rose. "There's still the matter of Leadford's blackmail."

Victor followed him to the door. "I've been thinking about that. What do you suppose the Church's views are on blackmail and extortion? I heard him threaten Thea too."

James paused in putting on his hat. A slow, pleased smile turned his mouth upward.

"Why, I should say, every bit as unfavorable as embezzlement."

His smile victorious, Victor held the door open. "I think it's time we paid Leadford a visit."

Victor sat in the parsonage's cozy, outdated parlor sipping tea with Mrs. Brentwood and James. He'd taken a cursory glance at the Church's ledgers earlier. They were a muddle, but even so, he identified several instances of altered amounts, two as recent as this past week. He couldn't be sure, of course, but to his eye, it appeared more than one person had changed the entries dating back at least two years.

Someone might argue one or more of the women in the household had abetted the reverend, but more likely it was the curate in charge of bookkeeping.

If all went as Victor had planned, it wouldn't matter.

James thought Victor's scheme feasible as well.

"Your daughters aren't at home?" Victor asked, even as he sought Thea. Like a ray of sunshine, she always brightened any room she was in and filled him with a peace he found nowhere else. "I should like them to be present as well."

"Theadosia is inquiring if our recent purchases might be returned." Faint color lined Mrs. Brentwood's cheekbones as she brushed a crumb off her lap, her hand unsteady. "When I saw you ride up, I sent Jessica out the back entrance to retrieve her sister."

The poor woman looked like she hadn't slept either. How could she when her husband faced disgrace, scandal, and imprisonment, and a blackmailing rotter had demanded her daughter marry him?

"I expect my husband and Mr. Leadford home for the midday meal at any moment," she said. "Mr. Cox suffered a broken leg when he was thrown from his horse yesterday. Oscar does so enjoy bringing a bit of encouragement to those convalescing."

Sugar tongs in hand, she wrinkled her forehead.

"Did I already add sugar to my tea?"

She spoke to herself, and Victor met James's concerned gaze over her bent head.

With a little shrug, she added a fifth lump of sugar, and stirring her very sweet tea, gave them a fatigued smile.

"Oscar truly loves his parishioners, but I expect you're here to discuss that other unpleasantness, aren't you?"

"When everyone is present since it concerns them as well." Victor forced himself to drink the tea, but after the coffee this morning and two tankards of ale, his stomach protested against any more liquids.

"He'll have to resign, won't he?" Mrs. Brentwood looked first to her son and then to Victor. Her bravado slipped, and she gave a defeated little nod. "Yes. Of course he will. I presumed as much."

She touched a bent knuckle to the corner of her eye.

"He has no choice, Mama." James leaned forward, his elbows on his knees. "If Father's to be granted any grace, he must show true humility and remorse. He can never be trusted with a parish again. You must know he'll be defrocked."

The column of her throat worked, and she blinked several times.

"Yes. I thought so. I'm not sure what we'll do, but Oscar will think of something."

If he wasn't rotting in a prison cell.

Victor stared into his cooling brew. He'd been mulling over that very detail. Everything depended on whether Brentwood was brought up on charges. And that depended on whether Leadford could be convinced to keep quiet.

He permitted a satisfied upturn of his mouth. He believed he had just the means to ensure Leadford did.

A ruckus in the entry and a door *clunking* shut announced someone had returned.

"Have you decided yet, Oscar?" Leadford asked. "I really do think it best if I procure a special license and the ceremony takes place at once."

"That worm cannot marry my Thea, James," Mrs. Brentwood whispered fiercely. A mother's protectiveness rendered her voice and expression fierce. "He simply can *not*."

"Mrs. Brentwood, he shan't," Victor said. "I need you to trust me in this."

Features tight, her worried brown eyes so like Thea's, she gave a quick nod.

"I'm not discussing that right now, Hector." Disdain riddled the reverend's hushed voice. "Besides, it appears we have callers."

Mrs. Brentwood rose and sailed to the entrance.

"Oscar, the Duke of Sutcliffe is here, as is James. I've sent Jessica for Theadosia. His Grace wishes to speak to all of us."

"I'll just bet he does," Leadford all but sniggered. A moment later, he swaggered into the parlor, greeting Victor and James with a surly, "Gentlemen."

He helped himself to a handful of biscuits before flopping into an armchair. No doubt he thought he controlled the situation. Was he in for a nasty surprise.

Jubilation thrummed through Victor, blaring triumph's fanfare in his blood.

Mrs. Brentwood sent Leadford a censuring frown as she returned to her seat and lifted the pot.

"Tea, Oscar?"

"No, thank you." Mr. Brentwood gave Victor the briefest tilt of his chin in greeting. Mortification fairly radiated off of his stiff form. "James, what goes on here?"

James stopped drumming his fingertips on the arm of the settee. "The Duke and I—"

More commotion in the entry announced the girls' return.

Thea glided in, her arms laden with packages wrapped in brown paper and tied with strings. She stalled at the entrance when she saw everyone.

Mrs. Brentwood took in the bundle Thea laid atop the table near the door. Her welcoming smile dissolved. "No luck, dearest?"

Again, Thea's gaze swept the room's occupants, her delicate nose flaring as she encountered Leadford's bold regard.

She sliced him a frigid look.

"I'm afraid not, Mama."

"Oh, I hope the tea is hot." Jessica, her cheeks whipped rosy by the wind, looped her hand through

Thea's elbow and guided her to the settee that Victor sat upon.

"I'm quite chilled," she said, perching on the arm of her mother's seat instead of taking the only remaining chair beside Leadford.

Even as she accepted her steaming cup of tea, the tumultuous clouds outside released their generous contents.

"Was there ever such a cool summer?" Mrs. Brentwood idly remarked to no one in particular.

With a graceful swish of skirts, Thea sank onto the cushion beside Victor. After balancing her umbrella against the seat, she declined tea with a small shake of her head as she removed her bonnet. Not the cheerful one with the blue roses, but a frumpy straw affair with but a single green ribbon frayed at the edges.

"What was so urgent Jessica had to drag me home before I finished my errands?"

Everyone looked to Victor. He hooked his ankle over his knee and examined the fingernails on his left hand. "We are all aware that Leadford's blackmailing Mr. Brentwood, are we not?"

Everyone gave a cautious nod.

The reverend's face reddened, but Leadford didn't even have the decency to look abashed.

He lifted a shoulder, his manner cockily confident.

"Don't make me out to be the villain. I'm simply taking advantage of an opportunity to better my situation." He flicked his biscuit-crumb covered fingers toward Mr. Brentwood. "He has only himself to blame for stealing Church monies."

Thea grasped the handle of her umbrella.

Was she contemplating thwacking Leadford?

Victor would quite like to see that.

Lips pressed together, the reverend remained silent, his focus on his folded hands. Even Victor felt a dash of empathy for the chagrined man.

"When was the last time you altered the books, Mr. Brentwood?" he asked.

Surprised, the cleric blinked. His thick, silver-peppered brows furrowed in thought, he scratched his chin. "At least four months ago. I've been saving what I took and slowly doling it out so it wouldn't be obvious to Marianne."

"Four months ago, you say? Then why do the ledgers clearly show at least two adjustments last week?" Victor slash Leadford a what-do-you-have-to-say-about-that glare.

Straightening his spine in indignation, Mr. Brentwood turned his contemptuous regard upon Leadford. "You accuse me, threaten to ruin my life, blackmail me and coerce me to agreeing to let my precious daughter marry you, and then you commit the same sin?"

For the first time, Leadford looked uncomfortable. He wet his lower lip and shifted his feet. "No, no, I haven't." He pointed at Brentwood. "You're the only one who's guilty of that crime."

Victor suspected the previous curate might've had sticky fingers too, for Brentwood clearly had no idea how to keep books properly. A wonder there hadn't been consequences before now.

It didn't matter. Victor intended to repay every penny.

"I have a proposition. One that I think will work to everyone's benefit." He gave Theadosia a reassuring smile.

A tiny glimmer of something shimmered in her eyes for a moment, then faded.

A tendril had come lose when she removed her hat, and the wavy strand teased her ear. Was her hair half as soft as it looked? He longed to find out, to see the mass unbound and draped about her shoulders and back.

If all went well, he would.

"Do you trust me, Thea?"

Her pretty eyes went soft around the edges. "Of course I do."

"I think you're forgetting who has the upper hand here." Leadford made a rude noise, his bluster returning. "There's nothing you can do or say—"

Victor raised his hand. "Hear me out."

"Yes, do hush, Mr. Leadford," Mrs. Brentwood said. "I've had quite enough of you. In fact," she slid her husband a sideways glance, then squared her shoulders. "In fact, you need to be gone from All Saint's within the hour. We'll take our chances with the courts and the Church."

Leadford's mocking laugh rang out. "You'd subject your daughters to prison? Do you know what they do to pretty young women there? Shall I tell you?"

He'd probably enjoy the telling, the depraved sot.

"Enough. It won't come to that." Victor stood and, hands clasped behind his back, paced away. "I'll repay all of the missing funds. I don't care who took them, but I shall assure the books are balanced down to the last groat."

Jessica gripped her mother's hand, and hope lit Mrs. Brentwood's wan features.

"As generous as that is, Your Grace," Mr. Brentwood said, "it doesn't excuse the fact that I committed a crime and I've a gambling addiction."

"Exactly." Leadford pounced, claws barred. "If the Diocese were aware, you'd be defrocked, and you'd face a prison sentence or hanging."

James jerked his head in Leadford's direction. "Men do not hang for theft, you dolt."

"He'd still go to prison. Probably die there. Then what of his wife and daughters?" Leadford's left eye twitched. A dead giveaway he was nervous as hell.

Victor laughed and splayed a hand on his nape. "You really didn't think this through, did you? James would care for his family, naturally."

Leadford pushed to his feet. "I'm going to write an overdue letter. We'll just see who's laughing then."

"You might want to rethink that, Leadford," James said, before yawning behind his hand. "Do you honestly think the courts or the Church will look kindlier on an extortioner? I'm a barrister. I should know. Particularly since it can be argued you also stole from the Church."

Victor patted his coat pocket. "I have a letter here from my friend, the Duke of Westfall. He did a little snooping around for me. I was actually surprised to hear from him so soon. Seems you were a rather unsavory chap in your last two positions. The Church didn't want a scandal so they moved you on each time. Theadosia is not the first young woman to spurn your attentions, is she?"

"Oh, well done you, Your Grace." A fragile smile curved Theadosia's mouth, and her face glowed with optimism.

"Well, well, what an interesting turn of events." James leaned back and folded his arms. "The self-righteous buggar has a history *he'd* rather not be made known."

"Nothing was ever proven." Leadford plucked at his collar, his face a rather peculiar shade of greyish-green.

"Here's what's going to happen, Leadford." Victor rested his hands on the back of the settee, Thea's satiny neck mere inches away. He gripped the wood tighter.

"I'm going to give you a large purse, and you're going to disappear. And that means you'll never accept a clergyman's position again. If I ever see you or even hear your name whispered again, friends of mine with questionable connections might be encouraged to abduct you and maroon you on a remote—a very, *very* remote—tropical island."

Leadford's jaw sagged to his chin, and he deflated like an impaled hot air balloon. He looked from person to person, then wet his lips.

"Fine. I'll go. But only because you threatened

me."

Victor hitched a shoulder. "Just as you threatened Theadosia and her family."

"When do I get my money?" Leadford asked.

Greedy sod.

"Be at the Blue Rose Inn at Essex Crossings at . . ." Victor withdrew his timepiece. "Four o'clock."

After a glare all around, Leadford stomped from the room.

Mr. Brentwood sighed then pushed to his feet. "I'm grateful you've rid us of that vermin, Your Grace. And I'm indebted to you for your offer to repay the funds I borrowed."

Still couldn't admit he'd stolen the money, could he?

"You didn't borrow them, Papa. You stole them and used Mama, Jessica, and me as an excuse to do so." Theadosia's quiet but resolved voice pinned him to the floor.

"You're right, Theadosia." His shoulders drooped, and he seemed to shrink into himself at her censure. "Nonetheless, I humbly accept your offer, Your Grace.

I've no wish to spend the remainder of my life in prison, even though it's what I deserve for betraying my flock and my family. If you'll excuse me, I need to write a letter of resignation."

"Mr. Brentwood, *all* of the offers I made previously still stand, if you are willing to accept them." Victor re-pocketed his watch. "If I may be so bold, perhaps you might suggest in your letter that you persuaded me to restore the Church and parsonage as part of your recompense. And I, too, shall be writing a letter on your behalf."

"Thank you. Your generosity and kindness do you credit, and I do accept *all* of your proposals." The reverend's attention shifted to Theadosia. "Please forgive me, my dear. I've been unforgivably hard-hearted, selfish, and obstinate." He closed his eyes, anguish contorting his face. "And prideful. So blasted prideful."

In a flash, she was in his arms, hugging her father.

"Of course I forgive you, Papa. Does this mean we can see Althea again?" she asked swiping tears from her cheeks.

"Yes, if she can forgive a stubborn, foolish old man." Mr. Brentwood shuffled from the room, a broken man.

"Please excuse me, Your Grace. My husband needs me." After a brief curtsy, his wife swiftly followed him.

Victor turned to James and withdrew a sizable envelope from his pocket. "This is for Leadford. Will you meet him on my behalf? I also want an agreement in writing. I'm taking no chances with that wretch. Can you deal with that as well?"

"I'd be happy to, just to see the look on his face when I make him sign it." James rose and stretched. "I must say, I thoroughly enjoyed you taking that rotter down a few pegs." He reached for Jessica's hand. "Come, pet. I'm ravenous. Let's see what we can rummage up in the kitchen, shall we?"

Jessica smiled at Thea. "We can keep our new gowns after all. We won't have to attend the ball in our old frocks."

She accepted James's help, and then with a bounce in her step, they departed.

Thea canted her head, giving him a joyous smile.

"You're our hero, Victor. Yesterday, I believed there was no hope and today, you've set everything to rights."

Once again, his mother had been correct. Women adored heroes.

Her exquisite face radiated with love for him. It humbled and exhilarated at the same time.

How he'd resented coming back to Colchester, resented the stipulation in Father's will. As it turned out, Father had known what was best, even when Victor didn't.

Cupping her shoulders, he bent and kissed her petal-soft lips.

"Not everything, my love."

"What else is there?"

An endearing perplexed frown creased her forehead.

"There's the matter of a proper proposal after your father just agreed that I might." He fingered her tempting lock of reddish blond hair.

"He did no such thing."

"Oh, but he did. I said *all* of my offers still stood, and he said he accepted *all* of them."

She angled her head.

"Do you love me, Victor?"

"I do." He tweaked her nose. "I love you so much I cannot find adequate words. I told my mother this morning that I realized I did before I left three years ago. I also told her that I would marry no other save you and that if that meant I wasn't wed by my birthday, dear Cousin Jeffery would suddenly become a wealthy chap."

Tears sparkled in her eyes, and she grasped his lapels.

"Did you truly?" She leaned away, her expression wary. "Was the duchess upset about possibly losing her home?"

"On the contrary, my love. She ordered me to do whatever I must to save you." He kissed her nose. "I think she's already rather fond of you."

"Poor Jeffery. He'll be so very disappointed."

Thea twined her arms about Victor's neck.

He cocked a brow. "And why is that?"

"Because we'll be married by your birthday, silly man." She raised up on her toes, drawing his head downward. "Now kiss me, my dearest love."

"With pleasure, Duchess."

Victor grasped her waist and lifted her, sealing their troth with a kiss that branded both their souls.

Epilogue

Ridgewood Court, Masquerade Fairy-tale Ball
21 July, 1809

Searching for her husband of almost ten hours, Theadosia ran her fingers along the gold satin ribbon-covered handle of her masquerade mask. Several gentlemen whose names she couldn't recall in the flurry of introductions—except for the Dukes of Dandridge, Pennington, Westfall, and Bainbridge—had hustled him off toward the terrace after the first set.

Grinning, something he'd done most of the day, his hands palm upward and extended in resignation,

Victor had winked and allowed his mischievous friends to tow him away.

"I'll be back as soon as I can escape these rakes, Duchess."

Probably sampling a bottle of spirits whilst toasting—*or reproving*—his stupidity for jumping headlong into the parson's mousetrap less than a month after he'd returned to Colchester.

She and Victor hadn't had a moment alone the entire day. After the ceremony this morning, there'd been an extravagant breakfast, and the rest of the time had been filled with activities for the house party as well as guest after guest wishing them happy. And to think they had nearly a week more of this chaos before leaving for their wedding trip.

A smile tugged her lips upward.

Truth to tell, she didn't mind, for her dearest friends and Jessica were gathered around her, each resplendent in fanciful gowns of silk and satin. Her own fairy-tale confection, a purple and gold creation so divine she'd almost been afraid to wear it, shimmered with thousands of tiny seed pearls.

Victor had secretly commissioned it and surprised her with the gown this afternoon, along with a pair of golden slippers covered with hundreds of glass beads.

"For my very own Cendrillon," he'd said, gathering her into his arms for a spine-tingling kiss. "Have I told you how happy I am, my darling?"

"No more than I, Victor." She kissed the corner of his mouth. "It still feels like a dream, and I'm afraid I'm going to wake up."

"As long as you wake up beside me every day for the rest of my life." He gazed longingly at the enormous four-poster bed dominating her bedchamber. "If I wasn't determined to not rush our first joining, Duchess . . ."

His voice had gone low and husky, his eyes hooded with desire, and answering passion had warmed her blood.

She grabbed his hand, tugging him toward the bed. "We've hours before—"

After a short rap on her door, the bubbly lady's maid assigned to Theadosia barged in. The servant's eyes rounded in surprise, and a blush scooted up her already ruddy cheeks.

"Beg your pardon, Your Grace." She curtsied, her focus glued to the floor. "I didn't know you were here."

Sighing, he'd kissed Theadosia on the nose.

"I've just given my wife a new ball gown. Please see that the wrinkles are removed before tonight, and I want her hair worn down, please."

The extraordinary amethyst and diamond parure set Theadosia wore, complete with a tiara fit for a princess, had been another gift from him, delivered as she dressed for the ball. She did feel like royalty, and today had been nothing short of magical.

She'd been the one to suggest that they wed today to save her mother-in-law additional work preparing for a grand wedding. It also spared Theadosia's parents a great deal of awkwardness.

Papa had performed the ceremony, but neither he nor her mother were attending the ball. He'd vowed he didn't deserve the privilege, but more probably, humiliation kept him away, as well as a renewed oath to avoid gaming of any sort, including cards. The news of his resignation and the reason behind his hasty notice had traveled swiftly through Colchester and the surrounding area.

Next week her parents would sail to Australia, accompanying a shipload of convicts and soldiers. The Church had magnanimously offered her father a position there as vicar; no one else showed the least interest in such a remote, primitive post. He'd been so grateful not to be defrocked, he'd eagerly accepted, but only after asking if Jessica might live with Theadosia and Victor. He would not risk towing his unmarried daughter halfway across the world, exposing her to dangers unknown.

Althea and her family were expected in two days. Mama had wanted to see her daughter and grandchildren before sailing to Australia. Especially since she and Papa would be gone for three years; time enough for the gossip to settle.

Craning her neck, Theadosia searched the ballroom for Victor once more. Silly to miss him so much. Only a few minutes had passed.

"Thea, I think it was terribly rude of the Duke of

Bainbridge to commandeer Sutcliffe the way he did. Surely he knows a groom's place is at his bride's side on their wedding day." Jessica slipped her hand into the crook of Thea's arm. Wide-eyed and excited, she too scrutinized the ballroom, no doubt hopeful her dance card would be filled before evening's end.

"Don't fret, Jessica. It's just the way of men. They only think of themselves. He meant no offense. They never do." A tinge of bitterness crept into Nicolette's voice.

Her betrothed had tossed her over for an heiress two seasons ago. Ever since, she'd become a consummate flirt, gaining a reputation for crushing any man foolish enough to try to pay his addresses.

Nicolette brushed her gloved hands down the front of her embroidered white satin gown. The royal blue velvet half coat perfectly matched her eyes, which sparkled with mischief at the moment. "I don't recall ever being in the company of so many seductive scoundrels, do you, Gabriella and Ophelia? What great fun we'll have this week."

Wearing identical gowns, except for the color, the

twins shook their heads.

"No, not to mention so many devilish dukes," Ophelia said, a skeptical brow arched.

Mirroring her twin's action, Gabriella lifted a matching eloquent eyebrow. "Sutcliffe certainly travels in exclusive circles, Thea."

Like Theadosia, the twins had never left Colchester. They lived with their aged grandparents and rarely attended anything more exciting than a tea or church. To liven things up, they were known to switch identities every now and again. Few people, except their family and dearest friends, could tell them apart.

"Ah, there you all are at last. I almost despaired of finding you in this infernal crush. I suppose that means the ball is a smashing success." Everleigh Chatterton glided toward them, her silvery gown, trimmed in black satin, accenting her white blonde hair. She'd been widowed almost two years ago but still wore half-mourning colors right down to her jet and diamond locket and earrings, as well as her ebony silk gloves.

Theadosia suspected Everleigh's extended

mourning period had far more to do with discouraging the attention of besotted men attracted to the stunning beauty like bees to blossoms, rather than any lingering grief she felt for the loss of her much, *much* older and despised husband.

Jemmah, the Duchess of Dandridge and Rayne Wellbrook, Everleigh's step-niece, accompanied her. They smiled in greeting whilst vigorously waving their fans.

"Lord, but it's stifling," the Duchess of Dandridge said. Hers had been a fairy-tale match too.

Thea glanced from friend to friend, and finally to Jessica. If only they might have their happily-ever-afters as well someday.

She would pray they did.

The Duchess of Dandridge had the right of it, nonetheless. The ballroom had grown beastly hot in a short period. If only Thea might slip outdoors for a breath of fresh air, perhaps even run her hands through the fountain bubbling in the garden.

"Is that tall, dark man still behind me?" Everleigh murmured as she also flicked her horn *brisé* fan open.

Behind her silver mask, her jade green eyes sparked with annoyance.

An exotic looking gentleman followed her, accompanied by the Dowager Duchess of Sutcliffe and the banker Jerome DuBoise, her nearly constant companion since his arrival four days ago.

"Yes." Theadosia nodded, searching for an excuse to whisk her friend away. "Why don't we get some ratafia? I'm quite parched."

"Theadosia my dear, where's Sutcliffe off to? I thought for certain he'd stick to your side the entire evening." The dowager duchess fairly glowed under Mr. DuBois's obvious admiration.

"A few of his friends wanted to wish him happy." Thea returned her smile. Her mother-in-law already treated her like a beloved daughter. "I think it was really an excuse to indulge in a tot."

The dowager chuckled while gesturing to the tall man. "Do let me introduce Griffin, Duke of Sheffield. He's nephew to Mr. DuBois and quite the world traveler."

She efficiently finished the introductions, and after

the women curtsied, Everleigh half-turned away, just short of snubbing the duke. Her marriage truly had been an awful affair and had left hidden wounds she refused to speak about. Even though she was only three and twenty, she'd sworn off men and marriage.

"Another duke?" Ophelia whispered soto voce to her twin. "How many does that make? Five or six?"

The Duke of Sheffield flashed a dazzling smile, his teeth white against his tanned face.

"Actually, there are ten of us. Myself, Dandridge, Sutcliffe, Pennington, Bainbridge, Westfall, Kincade, Asherford, San Sebastian, and Heatherston. The last three aren't here, however, and Kincade and Heatherston are Scots. We met at *Bon Chance* several years ago, and have been the greatest of friends since."

Bon Chance?

Wasn't that the scandalous gaming hell run by Madam Fordyce?

"Oh my, ten you say?" Ophelia appeared suitably awed, while her unimpressed twin hunched a shoulder.

"They're just men, Ophelia," Gabriella said.

"I imagine you've a great many interesting stories

you could tell." Nicolette batted her eyelashes. She appeared such a coquette, but any man foolish enough to take the bait soon found himself verbally skewered.

"There's Sutcliffe now." A proud smile illuming her face, the dowager pointed her closed fan.

Theadosia's gaze tangled with Victor's across the room, deliciously irresistible in his formal togs, as he strode toward her. Several other gentlemen, including the other dukes, each with varying degrees of disinterest or boredom etched on their aristocratic features, also ambled toward the cluster of women.

She wasn't the least surprised the male guests flocked to her exquisite friends. They were in for a surprise though, for none of the women gave a rat's wiry tail about impressing peers, social position, or how many titles a man held. A rarity to be sure, but that was one of the reasons the women were such close friends.

After bowing, Victor pulled Theadosia to his side. "I beg your indulgence, but I'm abducting my bride for a waltz on the terrace. You ladies should also dance."

He sent a swift, stern look to the other males

standing there. "Gentlemen, behave."

He didn't even wait for a response, but whisked Theadosia out a side door. No sooner had they left the ballroom's noise and heat than he swept her into a secluded corner and into his arms, crushing her to his chest and kissing her like a man long-starved.

She opened her mouth, welcoming him in. Her hunger grew, desire sluicing through every pore. Pulling her mouth free, she panted against his neck.

"Darling, do we dare forego the rest of the ball?"

The temperature inside the ballroom was nothing compared to the scorching need blazing within her.

"I'm a duke. I would dare anything for you, Duchess." Victor released a raspy chuckle. "Come. There's a back entrance."

Like naughty children, they clasped hands and ran to the other side of Ridgewood. Less than ten minutes later, after a few stops to indulge in blood sizzling kissing, Victor opened her bedchamber door.

Theadosia gasped, slowly spinning in a circle.

Dozens of candles lit the chamber, the glow casting romantic shadows to the farthest corners. A cheery fire burned in the hearth, and on the table near the window, a bottle of champagne chilled in a bucket between plates of sweetmeats and dainties. But it was the bed that commanded her attention. The bedding had been pulled to the foot, and coral and peach rose petals covered the ivory satin sheets.

"Oh, Victor. Did you arrange this? It's so romantic."

She lifted up on her toes and pressed a kiss to the corner of his firm mouth.

"I did." He pivoted her to unlace her gown. "And I told your maid she wouldn't be needed."

He made short work of divesting Theadosia of her clothing, but when he reached to pull her chemise over her head, she crossed her arms and backed away.

"No, you undress now. I want to see you."

A lazy grin curled his mouth.

"Your every wish is my command."

She watched him in the looking glass as she removed the tiara and earrings, and was about to unclasp the necklace when he closed his hand over hers.

"Leave it on. I want you wearing it when I make love to you."

He lifted her hair, pressing hot kisses to her neck, and a low moan escaped her.

Meeting his searing gaze in the mirror, Theadosia swallowed.

Wearing only his trousers, he radiated masculine beauty. Hair black as midnight covered his sculpted chest, the fine mat disappearing into the vee at his waist.

This glorious man was her husband.

She turned, offering him a siren's smile. Gazes still locked, she untied the ribbons at her shoulders, allowing her chemise to settle at her feet.

Victor froze for an instant before he scooped her into his arms and strode to the bed. Reverently, as if she were as fragile as the petals he lay her on, he lowered her to the mattress.

He shucked his trousers and slid onto the bed. "Let me take you to paradise, darling."

"Oh yes, Victor." She eagerly curled into his side, and sometime later when the heavens burst behind her eyelids and her body quaked with bliss, she cried, "I love you."

"And I love you, Thea," he groaned, finding his own release.

When their breathing had returned to normal, Victor raised Theadosia's hand to his lips and kissed her fingertips.

"For as long as I have breath in my body, Theadosia, I shall love you. You are branded on my spirit. My soul is finally whole."

"As is mine." She traced a finger along his jaw. "I suppose we have Leadford to thank."

Victor skewed a brow in astonishment. "And precisely how do you figure that devil is in any way worthy of our thanks?"

"Because, husband dearest, he forced your hand." She nuzzled his chest, then giggled when he tickled her ribs.

"Vixen."

"Enough talk." She climbed atop him, relishing the sensation of his firm, sinewy body beneath hers. "Take me to heaven again."

About the Author

USA Today Bestselling, award-winning author COLLETTE CAMERON® scribbles Scottish and Regency historicals featuring dashing rogues and scoundrels and the intrepid damsels who re-form them. Blessed with an overactive and witty muse that won't stop whispering new romantic romps in her ear, she's lived in Oregon her entire life, though she dreams of living in Scotland part-time. A self-confessed Cadbury chocoholic, you'll always find a dash of inspiration and a pinch of humor in her sweet-to-spicy timeless romances®.

Explore **Collette's worlds** at
www.collettecameron.com!

Join her **VIP Reader Club** and **FREE newsletter**.
Giggles guaranteed!

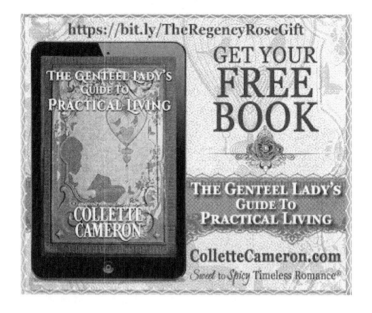

FREE BOOK: Join Collette's The Regency Rose®
VIP Reader Club to get updates on book releases,
cover reveals, contests and giveaways she reserves
exclusively for email and newsletter followers. Also,
any deals, sales, or special promotions are offered to
club members first. She will not share your name or
email, nor will she spam you.

http://bit.ly/TheRegencyRoseGift

From the Desk of Collette Cameron

Dearest Reader,

I'm so grateful you chose to read ONLY A DUKE WOULD DARE. I know you have many wonderful choices of historical romances to read, and I am honored you read the second book in my Seductive Scoundrel's Series.

Victor was introduced in A DIAMOND FOR A DUKE, and he was such a fun character, I couldn't wait to write his story. I wanted him to be flawed but redeemable; a hero who didn't really know what he wanted. Until he met Theadosia again, that is. She's all that I adore in a heroine: strong and intelligent, yet also a kind, considerate person.

Victor makes a cameo appearance in EARL OF WAINTHORPE, and you'll see more of Thea and her duke in the rest of the series as well.

The next book in the series is A DECEMBER

WITH A DUKE. Everleigh Chatterton is the heroine. I bet you can guess who the hero is!

Please consider telling other readers why you enjoyed this book by reviewing it. I adore hearing from my readers.

So, with that I'll leave you.

Here's wishing you many happy hours of reading, more happily-ever-afters than you can possibly enjoy in a lifetime, and abundant blessings to you and your loved-ones.

Collette Cameron

A Diamond for a Duke

Seductive Scoundrels, Book One

A dour duke and a wistful wallflower—an impossible match until fate intervenes one enchanted night.

Caution: This Historical Regency Romance contains a duke who literally thumbs his nose at society, a sweet and intelligent wallflower with a secret dream, a villainess worthy of a fairy tale, and two delightful match-making dowagers.

A dour duke.

Jules, the Sixth Duke of Dandridge, disdains Society and all its trappings, preferring the country's solitude and peace. Already jaded and cynical since the woman he loved died years ago, he's become even more so since unexpectedly inheriting a dukedom's responsibilities and finding himself the target of every husband-hunting vixen in London.

A wistful wallflower.

Forever in her stunning sister's shadow, Jemmah Dament has adored Jules from afar for years—since as children they were the best of friends. She daren't dream she can win a duke's heart any more than she hopes to escape the life of servitude imposed on her by an uncaring mother. Jemmah knows full well Jules is too far above her station. Besides, his family has already selected his perfect duchess: a poised, polished, exquisite blueblood.

But one enchanted night.

A chance encounter reunites Jules and Jemmah, resulting in a passionate interlude neither can forget. Jules realizes he wants more—much more—than Jemmah's sweet kisses or her warming his bed. He must somehow convince her to gamble on a dour duke. But can Jemmah trust a rogue promised to another? One who's sworn never to love again?

Enjoy the first chapter of

A Diamond for a Duke

Seductive Scoundrels, Book One

1

April 1809

London, England

A pox on duty.
A plague on the pesky dukedom too.

Not the tiniest speck of remorse troubled Jules, Duke of Dandridge, as he bolted from the crush of his godmother, Theodora, Viscountess Lockhart's fiftieth birthday ball—without bidding the dear lady a proper farewell, at that.

She'd forgive his discourtesy; his early departure too.

Unlike his mother, his uncles, and the majority of *le beau monde*, Theo understood him.

To honor her, he'd put in a rare social appearance and even stood up for the obligatory dances expected of someone of his station. Through sheer doggedness, he'd also forced his mouth to curve upward—good God, his face ached from the effort—and suffered the toady posturing of husband-stalking mamas and their bevy of pretty, wide-eyed offspring eager to snare an unattached duke.

Noteworthy, considering not so very long ago, Jules scarcely merited a passing glance from the same *tonnish* females now so keen to garner his favor. His perpetual scowl might be attributed to their disinterest.

Tonight's worst offender?

Theo's irksome sister-in-law, Mrs. Dament.

The tenacious woman had neatly maneuvered her admittedly stunning elder daughter, Adelinda, to his side multiple times, and only the Daments' intimate connection to Theo had kept him from turning on his heel at the fourth instance instead of graciously fetching mother and daughter the ratafia they'd requested.

A rather uncouth mental dialogue accompanied his march to the refreshment table, nonetheless.

Where was the other daughter—the sweet-tempered one, Miss Jemmah Dament?

Twiddling her thumbs at home again? Poor, kind, neglected sparrow of a thing.

As children and adolescents, he and Jemmah had been comfortable friends, made so by their similar distressing circumstances. But as must be, they'd grown up, and destiny or fate had placed multiple obstacles between them. He trotted off to university— shortly afterward becoming betrothed to Annabel—and for a time, the Daments simply faded from his and society's notice.

Oh, on occasion, Jules had spied Jemmah in passing. But she'd ducked her shiny honey-colored head and averted her acute sky-blue gaze. Almost as if she was discomfited or he'd somehow offended her.

Yet, after wracking his brain, he couldn't deduce what his transgression might've been.

At those times, recalling their prior relaxed companionship, his ability to talk to her about anything—or simply remain in compatible silence, an odd twinge pinged behind his ribs. Not regret exactly, though he hardly knew what to label the disquieting sensation.

Quite simply, he missed her friendship and company.

Since Theo's brother, Jasper, died two years ago, Jules had seen little of the Daments.

According to tattle, their circumstances had been drastically reduced. But even so, Jemmah's absence at routs, soirees, and other *ton* gatherings, which her mother and sister often attended, raised questions and eyebrows.

At least arced Jules's brow and stirred his curiosity.

If Jemmah were present at more assemblies, perhaps he'd make more of an effort to put in an appearance.

Or perhaps not.

He held no illusions about his lack of social acumen. A deficiency he had no desire to remedy.

Ever.

A trio of ladies rounded the corner, and he dove into a niche beside a vase-topped table.

The Chinese urn tottered, and he clamped the blue and white china between both hands, lest it crash to the floor and expose him.

He needn't have worried.

So engrossed in their titillating gossip about whether Lord Bacon wore stays, none of the women was the least aware of his presence as they sailed past.

Mentally patting himself on the back for his exceptionally civil behavior for the past pair of vexing hours, Jules permitted a self-satisfied smirk and stepped back into the corridor. He nearly collided with Theo's aged mother-in-law, the Dowager Viscountess Lockhart, come to town for her daughter-in-law's birthday.

A tuft of glossy black ostrich feathers adorned her hair, the tallest of which poked him in the eye.

Hell's bells.

"I beg your pardon, my lady."

Eye watering, Jules grasped her frail elbow, steadying her before she toppled over, such did she sway.

She chuckled, a soft crackle like delicate old lace, and squinted up at him, her faded eyes, the color of weak tea, snapping with mirth.

"Bolting, are you, Dandridge?"

Saucy, astute old bird.

Nothing much escaped Faye, Dowager Viscountess Lockhart's notice.

"I prefer to call it making a prudently-timed departure."

Which he'd be forced to abandon in order to assist the tottering dame back to her preferred throne—*er, seat*—in the ballroom.

He'd congratulated himself prematurely, blast it.

"Allow me to escort you, Lady Lockhart."

He daren't imply she needed his help, or she'd turn her tart tongue, and likely her china-handled cane, on him too.

"Flim flam. Don't be an utter nincompoop. You mightn't have another opportunity to flee. Go on with you now." She pointed her cane down the deserted passageway. "I'll contrive some drivel to explain your disappearance."

"I don't need a justification."

Beyond that he was bored to his polished shoes, he'd rather munch fresh horse manure than carry on anymore inane conversation, and crowds made him nervous as hell.

Always had.

Hence his infrequent appearances.

Pure naughtiness sparked in the dowager's eyes as she put a bony finger to her chin as if seriously contemplating what shocking tale she'd spin.

"What excuse should I use? Perhaps an abduction? *Hmph*. Not believable." She shook her head, and the ostrich feather danced in agreement. "An elopement? No, no. Won't do at all. Too dull and predictable."

She jutted her finger skyward, nearly poking his other eye.

"Ah, ha! I have just the thing. A scandalous

assignation. With a secret love. Oh, yes, that'll do nicely."

A decidedly teasing smile tipped her thin lips.

Jules vacillated.

She was right, of course.

If he didn't make good his escape now, he mightn't be able to for hours. Still, his conscience chafed at leaving her to hobble her way to the ballroom alone. For all of his darkling countenance and brusque comportment, he was still a gentleman first.

Lady Lockhart extracted her arm, and then poked him in the bicep with her pointy nail.

Hard.

"Go, I said, young scamp." Only she would dare call a duke a scamp. "I assure you, I'm not so infirm that I'm incapable of walking the distance without tumbling onto my face."

Maybe not her face, but what about the rest of her feeble form?

Her crepey features softened, and the beauty she'd once been peeked through the ravages of age. "It was good of you to come, Dandridge, and I know it meant the world to Theodora." The imp returned full on, and she bumped her cane's tip against his instep. "Now git yourself gone."

"Thank you, my lady." Jules lifted her hand, and after kissing the back, waited a few moments to assess her progress. If she struggled the least, he'd lay aside his plans and disregard her command.

A few feet along the corridor, she paused, half-turning toward him. Starchy silvery eyebrow raised, she mouthed, "Move your arse."

With a sharp salute, Jules complied and continued to reflect on his most successful venture into society in a great while.

Somehow—multiple glasses of superb champagne might be attributed to helping—he'd even managed to converse—perhaps a little less courteously than the majority of attendees, but certainly not as tersely as he was generally wont to—with the young bucks, dandies, and past-their-prime decrepitudes whose trivial interests consisted of horseflesh, the preposterous wagers on Whites's books, and the next bit of feminine fluff they might sample.

Or, in the older, less virile coves' cases, the unfortunate women subjected to their lusty ogling since the aged chaps' softer parts were wont to stay that way.

Only the welcome presence of the two men whom Jules might truly call 'friend,' Maxwell, Duke of Pennington, and Victor, Duke of Sutcliffe, had made the evening, if not pleasant, undoubtedly more interesting with their barbed humor and ongoing litany of drolly murmured sarcastic observations.

Compared to that acerbic pair, Jules, renowned for his acute intellect and grave mien, seemed quite the epitome of frivolous jollity.

But, by spitting camels, when his uncles, Leopold and Darius—from whom his middle names had been derived—had cornered him in the card room and demanded to know for the third time this month when he intended to do his *ducal duty*?

Marry and produce an heir...

Damn their interfering eyes!

Jules's rigidly controlled temper had slipped loose of its moorings, and he'd told them—ever so calmly, but also enunciating each syllable most carefully lest the mulish, bacon-brained pair misunderstand a single word—"go bugger yourselves and leave me be!"

He'd been officially betrothed once and nearly so a second time in his five-and-twenty years. Never again.

Never?

Fine, maybe someday. But not to a Society damsel and not for many, *many* years or before *he* had concluded the parson's mousetrap was both necessary and convenient. Should that fateful day never come to pass, well, best his Charmont uncles get busy producing male heirs themselves instead of dallying with actresses and opera singers.

Marching along the corridor, Jules tipped his mouth into his first genuine smile since alighting from his coach, other than the one he'd bestowed upon Theo when he arrived. Since his affianced, Annabel's death five years ago, Theo was one of the few people he felt any degree of true affection for.

Must be a character flaw—an inadequacy in his emotional reservoir, this inability to feel earnest emotions. In any event, he wanted to return home early enough to bid his niece and ward, Lady Sabrina Remington, good-night as he'd promised.

They'd celebrated her tenth birthday earlier today, too.

Jules truly enjoyed Sabrina's company.

Possibly because he could simply be himself, not Duke of Dandridge, or a peer, or a member of the House of Lords. Not quarry for eager-to-wed chits, a tolerant listener of friends' ribald jokes, or a wise counselor to troubled acquaintances. Not even a dutiful nephew, a less-favored son, a preferred godson, or at one time, a loving brother and wholly-devoted intended.

Anticipation of fleeing the crowd lengthening his strides, he cut a swift glance behind him, and his gut plummeted, arse over chin, to his shiny shoes.

Blisters and ballocks.

Who the devil invited *her*?

Printed in Great Britain
by Amazon